D0615354

Tartarin of Tarascon

ALPHONSE DAUDET

TRANSLATED BY J. M. COHEN

LITHOGRAPHS BY

M. LIN-DESPORTES

The Folio Society
London 1968

Binding design by John Lawrence

Set in 11 on 13 point Garamond and
printed by Butler and Tanner Ltd, Frome
Illustrations printed by The Baynard Press Ltd, London
Bound by W & J Mackay and Co Ltd, Chatham

Contents

Illustrations

Introduction

Alphonse Daudet, 1840–97, was a professional writer in the same sense as Charles Dickens. Dickens in fact after reading Daudet's first novel, a partial autobiography with resemblances to *David Copperfield*, referred to Daudet as his 'little brother in France' and followed his career with interest. Daudet wrote novels on a number of themes rooted in his own life experience. *Sappho* retold in fictional form a long ago love affair in Bohemian Paris. *Le Nabab* portrayed the Duc de Morny under whom Daudet served as secretary and *L'Immortel* tells the tale of a candidate for the Académie Française, a body which Daudet was too independent to stand for. One of his prime interests was the question of the Midi. Born at Nîmes, the son of an unsuccessful silk merchant, he taught for a while before coming to Paris to make a career as a writer. The Midi was undergoing a movement of intellectual revival called the Félibrige. The poet Frédéric Mistral was the leader of a group which was trying to revive the Provençal language. Daudet saw in himself all the characteristics of a southerner and in Tartarin de Tarascon drew a superb comic figure to represent that exuberance and imagination which he associated with the Midi. Its most characteristic expression was the *galéja*, which Daudet described in his foreword to the book written for its inclusion in his collected works:

'There is in the language of the poet Mistral, a word which comprises and defines clearly a whole instinct of the race: *galéja*, to joke, to make fun. And it conveys to the mind the flash of irony, the sparkle of malice, shining in the depths of the Provençal eyes. *Galéja* recurs on all occasions in the conversation, in the form of a verb or substantive. "*Vessés pàs? Es uno galéjado*. Don't you see? It is only a joke. *Taisoté galéjaïré*. Hold your tongue, you joker." But to be *galéjaïré* does not exclude from the character either kindness or tenderness. They amuse themselves, *té!* they must laugh....

'I too am a *galéjaïré*. In the fogs of Paris, in the splashing of her mud, in the sadness lurking in a great city, I may perhaps have lost the taste and faculty of laughter; but in reading *Tartarin*, any one may see that there then remained in me a store of gaiety which promptly broke forth in the glorious sunlight of "*down there*".'

Tartarin the lion hunter is rich in *galéja*. He boasts, he romances. But at the same time he turns a humorous eye on the oddities of the contemporary scene: the provinciality of his home town and the shabbiness of the French colonial adventure in Algeria. For it is to Algeria that Tartarin journeys in search of the 'King of Beasts'. Tartarin is in the succession of great comic characters from Gargantua—Anatole France noted the resemblance—by way of Don Quixote and Sancho Panza, Falstaff and Mistress Quickly to Pickwick. His adventures are absurd. His tales are largely untrue but then is not a lie itself something of a *galéja*? Daudet himself asks the question in a conversation recorded in the biography by his son Léon:

'Is it fair to call a man a liar, who intoxicates himself with his own talk, who, without any low motive, without a thought of deception, of guile, of profit, tries to beautify his own existence and that of others with stories which he knows to be imaginary, but would like to be true or probable? . . . Besides, among men of the Midi nobody is deceived. Each privately corrects the falsified proportions. It is all a matter of reduction to the proper terms.'

The proper terms were between a naturalistic novel and a fantasy. Daudet attached himself to the naturalistic school of Zola and in drawing the port of Marseilles, even in Tartarin, practised the art of naturalistic description. But Tartarin himself bursts the bonds of naturalism. He appears to have no relatives, his source of income is unknown, and we do not know how he acquired his vast collection of savage weapons. In Tarascon itself, nothing happens to him, but once he crosses the Mediterranean, adventures come thick and fast. Suddenly he falls in love, lives with a mistress, travels in search of lions, acquires a camel and returns with a reputation which, in the spirit of *galéja*, rests on precisely those deeds which he never succeeded in performing.

Tartarin de Tarascon was written in the year 1868 and met with nothing but misfortune. It was first serialized in a periodical whose largely working-class readership did not appreciate Daudet's humour. He then transferred it to *Le Figaro*, one of whose editors had served in Algeria and disliked Daudet's jokes at the expense of the colonial administration. He chopped Daudet's contributions into such small parts that the readers hardly noticed them. Then came the Franco-Prussian war in which Daudet served and from which he emerged saddened by the defeat and the Paris Commune. In 1872 *Tartarin* was published as a book, but in the meantime he had been threatened by a family called Barbarin—in the original version his hero was called by this name—who happened to live at Tarascon. Daudet had therefore to change his hero's name to the one that is now famous. He did not know Tarascon except as the name of a railway station, but its habitants and indeed many other patriotic southerners threatened him with vengeance. They considered themselves insulted, pilloried, mocked, but in the end the book was accepted and enjoyed and Tartarin became a proverbial figure. Indeed Daudet revived him in a second novel, *Tartarin sur les Alpes*, 1895, in which he made fun of mountaineers and the tourist trade which was just beginning in Switzerland. But this is not quite the old Tartarin of whom Daudet wrote in the foreword from which I have already quoted:

'My emotion is always the same, when *à propos* of some passer-by, one of the thousand marionettes of our human comedy, political, artistic, or of the world, I hear it said, "He is a Tartarin . . ." A thrill runs through me then, the proud thrill of a father, hidden amongst the crowd who applaud his son, and who, all the time, is longing to exclaim, "That is my boy!".'

Tartarin de Tarascon, like all Daudet's books, was translated and enjoyed in England soon after its first publication. Now, three-quarters of a century later, the old translation appears a bit tarnished. I send him out in new English dress confident that his *galéja* will amuse present-day readers as much as they amused their grandfathers.

J M COHEN
Knappswood, July 1967

First Episode

At Tarascon

The Garden with the Baobab Tree

My first visit to Tartarin of Tarascon marks an epoch in my life which I shall never forget. Though it may have been twelve or fifteen years ago it remains more clearly in my memory than the events of yesterday.

The bold Tartarin then lived on the edge of the town, in the third house on the left as you came in from Avignon. A pretty little villa in the local style with a garden in front, a balcony behind, dazzling white walls and green shutters, and on the doorstep a cluster of young bootblacks playing hopscotch or sleeping in the full sunlight with their heads on their blacking boxes.

From the outside, the house did not look remarkable.

You would *never* have believed you were facing a hero's home. But once you went in, lord bless my soul!

The whole place had a heroic look, from the cellar to the attic, even the garden.

Tartarin's garden! There wasn't another like it in the whole of Europe. Not a single native tree, not one familiar flower. Every plant was exotic: nothing but gums, calabash trees, cotton-woods, mangoes, banana-palms, date-palms, prickly pears, cacti, Indian figs. You would have thought yourself thirty thousand miles from Tarascon, in the heart of Central Africa. None of these plants, of course, were their natural size. The coconut palms were hardly bigger than beetroots, and the baobab tree (*arbos gigantea*—the giant) was easily contained by a mignonette pot. But it was quite a sight for Tarascon, all the same, and the townspeople who were permitted the honour of gazing on Tartarin's baobab tree on Sundays came away full of admiration.

Imagine my feelings that day as I crossed this marvellous garden! But they changed entirely when I was shown into the hero's study.

His study, which was one of the sights of the town, was at the end of the garden. Its glazed door opened straight on to the baobab.

Picture a large apartment, its walls covered from floor to ceiling with firearms and swords of every kind from every country in the world: carbines, rifles, blunderbusses, Corsican and Catalan knives, bayonets, daggers, krisses from Malaya, arrows from the Carib tribes, flint arrowheads, knuckle-dusters, life-preservers, Hottentot clubs, lassoos from Mexico—more weapons than I can name.

On this whole collection shone a full fierce sunlight which made the steel blades and firearm butts sparkle and sent cold shivers up your spine. But you were a little reassured by the charming air of order and cleanliness that reigned throughout this arsenal. Everything was in its place, tended, dusted and labelled as if in a chemist's shop, and at various points hung warning cards, on which was written

Poisoned arrows. Do not touch.

or

Loaded weapons. Beware!

But for these cards I should not have dared to enter.

In the middle of the study was an occasional table, and on this table a decanter of rum, a Turkish tobacco pouch, the novels of Fenimore Cooper and Gustave Aimard, sportsmen's tales of bear hunts, falconry, elephant shooting, etc. Lastly at this table sat a small, fat, thick-set and red-faced man of between forty and forty-five with a short beard and flashing eyes. He was in his shirtsleeves and flannel breeches. In one hand he held a book, and with the other brandished a huge pipe with an iron stopper. And as he read some blood-curdling tale of scalp-hunters, he pushed out his lower lip in a terrifying grimace, which lent the honest face of this small-town rentier the same look of harmless ferocity that reigned throughout the house.

This was Tartarin, Tartarin of Tarascon, the great, bold and incomparable Tartarin of Tarascon.

A general Survey of the Town of Tarascon. Cap-shooting

At the time of which I am speaking Tartarin of Tarascon was not yet the Tartarin of today, the great Tartarin who enjoys such a reputation throughout southern France. Even at this epoch he was nevertheless already king of Tarascon. Let me tell how he won his kingdom.

In the first place you must know that everyone down there, great and small, is a Sportsman. Shooting has been a passion in those parts since those mythological days when Tarasque, the local dragon, flourished her tail in the town marshes and the inhabitants of the day organized drives against her. That, as you may guess, was a long time ago.

So every Sunday morning the whole of Tarascon takes up arms and leaves its gates, game-bag on back and gun in hand, with a straining of dogs and ferrets, and a clatter of bugles and hunting-horns. It is a superb sight. But unfortunately there is no game, absolutely none. Animals may be very stupid. But, as you can imagine, they finally took fright. For fifteen miles round Tarascon, burrows were empty, and nests forsaken. Not a blackbird, not a quail, not the tiniest leveret or so much as a sparrow.

The hills around Tarascon, with their scent of myrtle, lavender and rosemary, are very tempting; and those fine muscat grapes bursting with sweetness that grow along the banks of the Rhône, are devilish appetizing too. But on the other side is Tarascon and in the little world of fur and feather Tarascon has a very bad reputation. The very birds of passage have put a great cross against it on their route-maps, and when the wild duck, flying towards the Camargue in their long V-formations, see the town's spires from afar, the leader gives a loud cry of 'Tarascon! There is Tarascon.' And the whole flight swerves away.

In short the only game that remains in the district is one sly old hare, who miraculously escaped from the citizens' September massacres and who stubbornly goes on living there. This hare is very famous in Tarascon, and has been nicknamed *Lightning*. He is known to have his form on M. Bompard's land—and this, by the way, has doubled, even trebled the value of the fields—but no one has yet managed to catch him. At the present time, there are only two or three madmen who persist in chasing him. The rest have resigned their interest, and *Lightning* has long ago passed into the realm of local superstitions, though Tarasconians are not very superstitious by nature and eat swallows* in a thick sauce when they find any.

* The swallow is Our Lady's bird. To eat it brings bad luck.

Well then, you will ask, since game is so rare at Tarascon, what do the local sportsmen do on Sundays?

What do they do? What indeed? That's a question. First, they go out into the open country, eight or nine miles from the town. They gather in knots of five or six, and lie down peacefully in the shade of a well-head, an old wall or an olive tree. Then they take a good hunk of boiled beef, some raw onions, a black pudding and some anchovies from their game-bags, and start an endless lunch, washed down with one of those pleasant Rhône wines that make you laugh and sing. After that, when they are well limbered up, they get on their feet, whistle their dogs, set their guns at half-cock, and start the shoot. That is to say, each gentleman takes his cap, flings it up with all his strength and fires at it while it is in the air with No 5, 6 or 2 shot, whichever is agreed. The man who scores most hits on his cap is proclaimed the sporting king, and re-enters Tarascon in triumph that evening, with his riddled cap on the muzzle of his gun, to the accompaniment of barking and fanfares.

Needless to say, there is a great trade in hunting-caps in the town. There are even some hatters who sell hunting-caps ready pierced and torn for the use of bad shots. But hardly anyone except Bézuquet the chemist has been known to buy one. It would be too disgraceful!

As a cap-shooter, Tartarin of Tarascon was unequalled. Every Sunday morning he set out with a new cap, and every evening returned with it in tatters. The attics of the house with the baobab were full of these glorious trophies. So all the men of Tarascon recognized him as their master, and as Tartarin knew the huntsman's code in every detail, and had read every treatise and manual on every possible sport from cap-shooting to hunting the Burmese tiger, these gentlemen made him their arbiter of cynegetics and brought all their disputes to him for settlement.

Between three and four o'clock every day, you would see a stout serious man, smoking a pipe and sitting in a green leather armchair in the middle of Costecalde the gunsmith's shop. The place was full of cap-shooters, who stood about and argued. This was Tartarin of Tarascon delivering judgements, a Nimrod and Solomon combined.

Naw! Naw! Naw! General Survey of Tarascon continued

Beside their passion for sport the lusty Tarasconians had another passion, a passion for sentimental ballads. The quantity of ballads consumed in this small district would defy belief. The old ballads that yellow elsewhere in the most ancient packages are to be found at Tarascon in all their youth and splendour. They are all there, every one of them. Each family has its favourite, and all the rest know which it is. It is well known throughout the town, for example, that at Bézuquet the chemist's it is

> Fair star of my dreams,
> Fair star that I adore

and at Costecalde the gunsmith's it is

> Will you come, will you come
> To my log-cabin land?

And at the official Registrar's

Oh, if I were invisible
I'm sure I'd not be seen

(*Comic ditty*)

And so on throughout Tarascon, two or three times a week the townsfolk will meet at each other's houses to sing them. And the strange thing is that they are always the same. In all the years that they have been singing to one another, these good Tarasconians have never had any inclination to make a change. The ballads are passed down in families from father to son, and no one touches them; they are sacred. And no one ever borrows his neighbour's. It would never occur to the Costecaldes to sing the Bézuquets' ballad nor to the Bézuquets to sing the Costecaldes'. And yet they must know each other's songs by heart since they have been singing them for forty years. Nevertheless, each family keeps its own, and everyone is content.

At ballads as at cap-shooting, Tartarin was the best in the town. His superiority over his fellow-citizens lay in the fact that Tartarin of Tarascon did not have a song of his own. He had them all. All! But it was the devil's own job to get him to sing them.

Retiring early from his drawing-room triumphs, the hero of Tarascon greatly preferred burying himself in his sporting books or spending an evening at the club to showing off before a piano manufactured in Nîmes between a pair of candles made at Tarascon. He found these musical displays beneath him. Sometimes, however, when there was a sing-song at Bézuquet the chemist's, he strolled in as if by accident and after a lot of persuasion consented to sing the duet from *Robert the Devil* with Madame Bézuquet senior. If you had not heard that, you had missed everything. For my part, if I were to live to a hundred, I should remember to my grave the great Tartarin solemnly walking up to the piano, leaning on it, pursing his lips, and beneath the green reflection from the bottles in the window trying to give his kindly face the fierce satanic expression of Robert the Devil. The moment he took his place beside the piano the whole room shuddered; everyone felt that great things were at hand. Then after a silence Madame Bézuquet senior began to her own accompaniment:

Robert, my love is thine
To thee I my faith did plight
Thou seest mine affright (*repeat*)
Mercy for thine
Own sake! Mercy for mine!

Then she would add in an undertone, 'Now you, Tartarin,' and Tartarin of Tarascon with outstretched arm and clenched fist, and nostrils quivering, would repeat three times in a mighty voice that echoed like a thunderclap in the bowels of the piano: 'No! No! No!' which like a true man of the Midi he pronounced, Naw, naw, naw! Upon which Madame Bézuquet senior sang again:

Mercy for thine
Own sake! Mercy for mine!

'Naw! naw! naw!' howled Tartarin at full pitch, and there the thing ended. . . . It was not very long, as you see. But it was so well produced, so well mimed and so diabolical that a shiver of terror ran through the chemist's shop and they made him repeat his Naw! . . . Naw! three or four times in succession.

Upon this Tartarin would mop his brow, smile to the ladies, wink to the men and, withdrawing after his triumph, set off for the club where he would remark with a little off-hand gesture: 'I have just been at the Bézuquets' singing the duet from Robert the Devil.'

And the cream of the joke was that he believed it.

They!

It is to these diverse talents that Tartarin of Tarascon owed his high position in the town. Moreover it is a fact that this devilish fellow had a way of captivating everybody. The army at Tarascon was all for him. The brave Major Bravida (retired), once superintendent of the clothing store, said of him: 'He's a sport!', and as you can imagine with his experience of providing them with uniforms he was a judge of men. The Bench was all for Tartarin too. Two or three times old President Ladeveze had said of him in a crowded court: 'He's a character!' Finally the people were all for Tartarin. His square build, his way of walking, his way of looking like a trumpeter's charger that did not fear the fray, and his reputation for heroism which came from goodness knows where, also a certain distribution of kicks and halfpence among the little ragamuffins who hung around his door, had made him the 'Milord' of the neighbourhood, the publicly acknowledged king of Tarascon. On Sunday evenings, when Tartarin came back from the shoot, with his cap on the muzzle of his gun and his fustian shooting-jacket tightly belted, some river-porters on the Rhône bank would bow respectfully and, glancing down at the huge biceps that swelled his arms, exclaimed to one another in admiration: 'Now there's a strong man for you! His muscles are *twice normal size.*'

Muscles. Nowhere but at Tarascon does one hear of things like that.

And yet, despite everything, with his numerous talents, his double-sized muscles, his popularity and the very precious respect of the brave Major Bravida, retired superintendent of the clothing store, Tartarin was not happy; this small-town life oppressed and stifled him. The great man of Tarascon was bored at Tarascon. The fact is that for a heroic nature like his, for a rash and adventurous soul who dreamt of nothing but battles, races across the pampas, mighty hunts, sands of the desert, hurricanes and typhoons, to go out cap-shooting every Sunday and pronounce judgements at Costecalde the gunsmith's for the rest of the week was hardly . . . Poor fellow! Great man though he was, this would in the end have been enough to make him die of consumption.

In vain to widen his horizons and make him occasionally forget the club and the market place, in vain did he surround himself with baobabs and other African plants, in vain did he pile up arms upon arms, Malayan kris on Malayan kris; in vain did he stuff his head with novel reading, trying like the immortal Don Quixote to free himself by the strength of his imagination from the pitiless claws of reality. Alas, all that he did to quench his thirst for adventures only served to increase it. The sight of all his weapons kept him in a perpetual state of fury and excitement. His rifles, his arrows, his lassoos cried: 'Battle! Battle!' The wind of distant travels blowing in the branches of his baobab put dangerous ideas in his head. And on top of all this, Gustave Aimard and Fenimore Cooper . . .

How often when he was alone on some oppressive summer afternoon, reading amongst his swords . . . how often did he get up with a roar? How often did he throw down his book and dash to the wall to unhook a set of arms?

Forgetting that he was at home in Tarascon with a kerchief on his head and in his indoor breeches, the poor man would translate his reading into action. Excited by the sound of his own voice, he would cry, brandishing an axe or a tomahawk: 'Now let them come, at last!'

Them? Who were they?

Tartarin himself did not clearly know. *They* were the attackers, the warriors, the scalpers, whooping and roaring as they came. *They* were the Sioux Indians dancing round the totem pole to which the unfortunate pale-face was lashed. *They* were the grizzly bears of the Rocky Mountains, swaying on their hind legs and licking themselves with bloody tongues. *They* were also the Touareg of the desert, the Malayan pirates, the bandits of the Abruzzi . . . *They*, in fact, were *they* . . . that is to say war, travel, adventure, glory.

But, alas, the fearless hero of Tarascon could summon and defy *them* to his heart's content. *They* never came. What business could *they* possibly have in Tarascon? Nevertheless Tartarin was always expecting *them*, particularly in the evening, on his way to the club.

Tartarin walks to his Club

A Knight Templar preparing to make a sortie against the besieging infidel, a Chinese *tiger* arming for battle, a Comanche warrior setting out on the warpath, all these were nothing compared with Tartarin of Tarascon equipping himself from head to foot to go to his club at nine in the evening, one hour after the evening bugle had sounded.

Clear decks for action! as they say in the navy.

In his left hand Tartarin carried a steel-pointed knuckle-duster and in his right a sword-stick; in his left pocket a life-preserver, in his right a revolver. Under his coat, between his shirt and his vest, he had a Malayan kris. But no poisoned arrows, of course, for these were unworthy weapons!

Before setting out, in the silence and darkness of his study, he spent a moment practising, parrying and lunging at the wall and limbering up his muscles. Then he picked up his master-key and crossed the garden, grave and unhurried, with the calm of an Englishman, with English coolness, gentlemen! That's the true courage.

On the further side of the garden he opened the heavy iron gate. He opened it forcefully and abruptly, so that it should bang against the outer wall. If *they* had been lurking behind it *they* would have been squashed to pulp.

Unfortunately *they* were not there.

Once the door was open, Tartarin went out and, after glancing to right and left, gave the key a double-turn. Not so much as a cat on the Avignon road. Closed doors, and no lights in the windows. Utter blackness except for the street-lamps blinking at intervals in the Rhône mist. Proudly and

calmly Tartarin of Tarascon walked through the night, beating regular time with his heels and striking sparks from the pavement with the ferrule of his stick. In avenues, streets and lanes alike he took care to keep in the middle of the road, an excellent precautionary measure, which enables you to see danger coming and also to avoid what is sometimes thrown into the street from Tarascon windows during the evening. Do not suppose when you see Tartarin exercising all this prudence that he was afraid. He was merely on his guard.

The best proof that Tartarin was not afraid is that instead of going to the club by the direct road, he went through the town, that is to say by the longest and darkest way, through a warren of wretched little streets at the end of which the Rhône can be seen shining with a sinister light. The poor man always hoped that at a turn in one of these cut-throat alleys, *they* would rush out of the shadows and fall on him from behind. *They* would have met with a warm reception, I promise you. But alas, by the mockery of fate never, absolutely never was Tartarin of Tarascon lucky enough to meet an awkward customer. Not even a dog, not even a drunkard. Nothing.

Sometimes however there were false alarms. The noise of steps, muffled voices. 'Look out!' Tartarin would say to himself and stand rooted to the spot, peering into shadows, sniffing the wind, and putting his ear to the ground in Indian fashion. The steps came nearer. The voices became distinct. *They* were upon him. With fiery eye and heaving chest, Tartarin was already drawing in on himself like a jaguar, preparing to leap forward uttering his war-cry, when suddenly from the heart of the shadows, he heard honest Tarascon voices calmly hailing him: 'Hi, you there! Surely it's Tartarin, isn't it? Good-night, old chap!'

Hell and damnation! It was Bézuquet and his family on their way home from singing their song at the Costecaldes' . . . 'Good-night! Good-night!' growled Tartarin, furious at his mistake and, wildly raising his stick, plunged into the night. On reaching the street in which the club stood the bold fellow delayed yet again to walk up and down before entering the door.

Finally, tired of waiting for *them* and certain that they would not show themselves now he threw a last glance of defiance into the shadows and muttered angrily: 'Nothing! Nothing! There's never anything at all!'

Whereupon the good man entered to play his game of bezique with the Major.

The two Tartarins

With this passion for adventures, this need for violent emotions, this weakness for voyages, expeditions and journeys into the devil's own country, how on earth was it that Tartarin had never left Tarascon?

For it is a fact that up to the age of forty-five the bold Tartarin had never slept out of Tarascon. He had not even made that famous journey to Marseilles that every good Provençal makes on coming of age. His knowledge did not extend beyond Beaucaire, and Beaucaire is no distance from Tarascon; there is only a bridge to cross. Unfortunately this confounded bridge has so often been blown down by storms, and is so long and frail, and the Rhône is so wide at that point that . . . well, you understand, Tartarin preferred *terra firma*.

It must certainly be admitted that our hero possessed two very distinct characters. 'I feel two men within me,' remarked some Father of the Church. He could as well have been speaking of Tartarin. For the bold Tarasconian had within him the soul of a Don Quixote, the same urges to chivalry, the same heroic ideals, the same weakness for the romantic and grandiose. But unfortunately he had not the body of that famous knight, that thin and bony body, that apology for a body on which material life had no hold, the body of one who could spend twenty nights without unbuckling his breastplate, and exist for forty-eight hours on a handful of rice. Tartarin's body, on the contrary, was a fine figure of a body, very fat, heavy, sensual, soft and sensitive, with middle-class habits and homely needs, a short paunchy body on the legs of the immortal Sancho Panza.

Don Quixote and Sancho Panza in the same man. You can imagine what a poor life they must have led together. What battles! What tearings of the flesh! What a fine dialogue Lucian or Saint-Evremond could have written, between the two Tartarins, Tartarin-Quixote and Tartarin-Sancho! Tartarin-Quixote enthusing over the tales of Gustave Aimard and crying, 'I shall set out!' and Tartarin-Sancho thinking only of his rheumatism saying, 'I shall stay behind!'

TARTARIN-QUIXOTE (*greatly excited*): Cover yourself in glory, Tartarin.

TARTARIN-SANCHO (*very calm*): Cover yourself in flannel.

TARTARIN-QUIXOTE (*still more excited*): Give me a double-barrelled gun. Give me daggers, lassoos, moccasins!

TARTARIN-SANCHO (*with increasing calm*): Give me a good

knitted waistcoat, and nice warm knee-caps! Give me a thick cap with ear-flaps!

TARTARIN-QUIXOTE (*beside himself*): A battle-axe! Give me a battle-axe!

TARTARIN-SANCHO (*ringing for the maid*): Jeannette, my chocolate!

Whereupon Jeannette appears with a good cup of hot chocolate, swirling and sweet to the nostrils, and some hot, succulent aniseed cakes which make Tartarin-Sancho chuckle so loudly that Tartarin-Quixote's cries are drowned. And this is the reason why Tartarin of Tarascon had never left Tarascon.

Big Business at Shanghai. Can Tartarin be an Impostor? The Mirage

Once however Tartarin had almost departed, had almost set out on a great journey. Garcio-Camus, the three brothers, natives of Tarascon established in business in Shanghai, offered him the managership of one of their offices there. Now that was really the life he wanted. Important business, an army of clerks to order about, commerce with Russia, Persia, Turkey in Asia, big business in fact. In Tartarin's mouth, the words big business sounded big indeed.

The house of Garcio-Camus had this additional advantage, that it sometimes received a visit from the Tartars. Then all doors were immediately shut. All the clerks seized their guns, the consular flag was run up, and Bang, bang! out of the windows upon the Tartars. There is no need to describe the enthusiasm with which Tartarin-Quixote leapt at this proposal. Unfortunately Tartarin-Sancho did not hear it with the same ears, and as he was the stronger party no arrangements could be made. The matter was much discussed in the town. Would he go? Wouldn't he go? 'I bet he does.' 'I bet he doesn't.' It was an event. In the end, Tartarin did not go. Nevertheless the story redounded greatly to his credit. To have gone to Shanghai and almost to have gone to Shanghai were for Tarascon much the same thing. There was so much talk of Tartarin's journey that it was finally believed that he had been and come back, and at the club in the evenings, gentlemen would ask him for information about life in Shanghai, the customs, the climate, opium and big business.

Being very well informed, Tartarin gladly gave them all the details they desired, and after some time the good man was himself not quite certain whether he had not in fact been there, so uncertain indeed that after telling the story of the Tartar raid for the hundredth time, he would find himself saying quite naturally: 'Then I armed the clerks, I raised the consular flag and, Bang! Bang! out of the windows.' The whole club shuddered as they listened.

Then your friend Tartarin was just a frightful liar . . . No, good gracious no! Tartarin was not a liar.

But he knew perfectly well that he had not been to Shanghai.

Yes, of course he did. Only . . . Only . . . Now listen to me. It is time we came to an understanding once and for all about this Northern belief that the men of the Midi are liars. There are no liars in the South neither at Marseilles nor Nîmes nor Toulouse nor Tarascon. The Southerner does not lie, he deceives himself. He does not always tell the truth but he believes he is doing so. His peculiar falsehood is not a falsehood. It is a kind of mirage. Yes, a mirage. And if you want to understand me, go down into the Midi and you will see for yourself. You will see that devilish country where the sun transforms everything and makes it bigger than its natural size. You will see those little hills of Provence that are no higher than the Butte Montmartre, but they will look to you enormous. You will see the Square House at Nîmes, a little doll's-house, and it will seem to you as big as Notre-Dame. You will see. If there is a liar in the Midi, it is only the sun. It exaggerates everything it strikes. What was Sparta in the days of its glory? *A scattered settlement*. And Athens? A second-class town at best. And yet in history they appear to us like—great cities. That is the work of the sun. Does it surprise you then that the same sun, falling on Tarascon, made Bravida, the retired superintendent of the clothing store, into the brave major of that name, a turnip into a baobab, a man who had failed to go to Shanghai into a man who had been there?

Mitaine's Menagerie. A Lion from the Atlas at Tarascon. A fearsome and solemn Confrontation

And now that we have shown you Tartarin of Tarascon as he was in his private life before glory kissed his brow and wreathed it with the eternal laurel, now that we have described this heroic life in modest surroundings, its joys and griefs, its dreams and hopes, let us hasten on to the great pages of its history, and to the singular event which gave the first impulse to that incomparable destiny.

On a certain evening at Costecalde the gunsmith's, Tartarin of Tarascon happened to be busy demonstrating to some sportsmen the workings of the needle-gun, then an entire novelty. Suddenly the door opened and a cap-shooter rushed wildly into the shop, crying 'A lion! A lion!' General astonishment, alarm, tumult and disorder. Tartarin fixed a bayonet. Costecalde rushed to shut the door. All clustered round the newcomer, questioned him, cross-questioned him, and this is what they heard: Mitaine's menagerie, on its way back from Beaucaire, had consented to make a stay of some days at Tarascon, and had just opened up in the Place du Château with a number of boa-constrictors, seals and crocodiles and a magnificent lion from the Atlas.

A lion from the Atlas at Tarascon! Never in human memory had such a thing been seen. Our brave cap-shooters looked proudly into each others' faces. Their manly features glowed, and congratulatory handshakes were silently interchanged in every corner of Costecalde's shop. The excitement was so great and unexpected that no one found a word to say.

Not even Tartarin. Pale and trembling, with his needle-gun still in his hands, he stood dazed in front of the counter. A lion from the Atlas, there, quite close, only two steps away! A lion! The fiercest and most heroic of animals, the king of beasts, the big game of his dreams, the chief actor, as you might say, in the ideal company that performed such grand dramas in his imagination. A lion! By all the gods, a lion!

And a lion from the Atlas to boot! It was more than the brave Tartarin could bear. Suddenly a rush of blood mounted to his cheeks. His eyes kindled. With one convulsive movement, he shouldered the needle-gun and, turning to the brave Major Bravida (retired), he exclaimed in a voice of thunder: 'Let us go and see him, major.'

'Hi, just a moment there! It's my needle-gun you're going off with,' cried the cautious Costecalde nervously. But Tartarin had already vanished round the corner, followed by all the cap-shooters proudly marching behind him. When they reached the menagerie they found plenty of people there already. Tarascon, with its population of heroes, had been too long deprived of spectacles and sensations. It had made an onslaught on Mitaine's tent and taken it by storm. Stout Madame Mitaine was delighted. In Kabyle dress, with arms bare to the elbow and iron rings round her ankles, holding a riding-whip in one hand and a chicken, plucked but still alive, in the other, the illustrious lady was doing the honours of the exhibits to the people of Tarascon and, as she too had *muscles twice normal size*, she was almost as much a success as the animals.

Tartarin's entrance with his gun on his shoulder cast a sudden chill. All those brave citizens who were calmly parading before the cages, without mistrust or the least idea of danger, gave a start of quite natural terror on seeing the great Tartarin enter the tent with his fearsome weapon. There must be something to be afraid of if that hero . . . In the twinkling of an eye the space in front of the cages was emptied of people. Children were crying in terror, ladies were eyeing the exit. Bézuquet slipped out, saying that he was going to fetch his gun.

Tartarin's attitude, however, gradually restored the general courage. Cool and with head held high, this bold citizen calmly made a tour of the tent, walking, without a pause, past the seal's tank, and casting a contemptuous glance at the long, sawdust-filled box in which the boa was digesting its raw chicken. Finally he came to rest in front of the lion's cage.

A terrible and solemn confrontation! The lion of Tarascon and the lion of Atlas face to face. On the one hand Tartarin standing with leg-muscles tense and both arms resting on his gun. On the other the lion, a gigantic lion crouching in the straw with blinking eyes, a brutish expression and his enormous tawny full-bottomed wig resting on his forepaws. They gazed at one another, both calm.

Then a strange thing occurred. Whether it was because he was annoyed by the needle-gun, or had scented the enemy of his tribe, the lion which had so far viewed the citizens of Tarascon with an expression of sovereign disdain, yawning in all their faces, suddenly became enraged. First he sniffed and gave a low growl, then he spread his claws and stretched out his paws, and then he got up, lifted his head, shook his mane, opened his huge jaws, and roared ferociously at Tartarin.

The response was a yell of terror. All Tarascon rushed wildly to the exit, women, children, river-porters, cap-shooters and the brave Major Bravida himself. Tartarin of Tarascon alone did not stir. He stood firmly resolute before the cage, with lightning in his eyes and that grimace all the town knew on his face. Slightly reassured by his attitude and the strength of the bars, the cap-shooters then rejoined their chief and heard him mutter, as he gazed at the lion: 'Now there's a beast that's worth hunting.' Tartarin of Tarascon said nothing more that day.

Strange Effects of the Mirage

Tartarin of Tarascon said nothing more that day. But the unfortunate man had already said too much. Next day, the only subject of conversation in the town was Tartarin's impending departure for Algeria to hunt the lion. You are all witnesses, dear readers, that the good man had never breathed a word about it. But you know the mirage . . . In short, all Tarascon was talking of nothing but his departure. On the street, in the club, at Costecalde's shop men went up to one another, saying excitedly: 'Tell me, I suppose you know the news?'

'Tell me, what news? Oh, about Tartarin's expedition, I suppose.'

At Tarascon all sentences begin with *Tell me*, which is pronounced *Termi*, and end with *I suppose*, which is shortened to *Is'pose*. And on that day in particular the *termis* and *Is'poses* were loud enough to shake the window-panes. No one in the town was more surprised than Tartarin himself to learn that he was leaving for Africa. But reflect on the nature of vanity! Instead of simply stating that he was not going at all, and had never had any intention of going, the first time someone spoke to him of his journey Tartarin said with a slightly evasive gesture: 'Aha, perhaps, really I can't say.' The second time, a little more accustomed to the idea, he answered: 'Very likely.' And the third time: 'Yes, of course. Certainly, I shall go.'

Finally at Costecalde's that evening, carried away by the egg nog, the lights and the congratulations, and elated by the way in which the town had received the news of his coming departure, the poor man formally declared that he was sick of cap-shooting and was shortly setting out to hunt the great lions of the Atlas. This declaration was greeted with mighty cheers followed by more egg nog, hand-shakings, back-slappings, and a serenade in front of the little house of the baobab, which went on till midnight.

Tartarin-Sancho was much displeased. The idea of travelling in Africa and hunting the lion made him shiver in anticipation. On returning home, while the serenade of honour was still sounding beneath the windows, he made Tartarin-Quixote a terrible scene, calling him a crackpot, a visionary, a rash and triple-dyed fool, and retailing to him in full detail all the disasters that awaited him on this expedition: shipwrecks, rheumatism, burning fevers, dysentery, the black plague, elephantiasis and all the rest.

In vain did Tartarin-Quixote swear not to do anything foolish, to keep well wrapped up and take everything that was necessary. Tartarin-Sancho refused to listen. The poor man saw himself already torn to pieces by lions and swallowed by desert sands like the late Cambyses, and the other Tartarin could only manage to appease him a little when he explained that nothing was to happen just now, that there was no hurry, and after all they had not departed yet.

It is quite obvious that no one sets out on such an expedition without making some preparations. Dash it all, a man must know where he is going. He cannot just fly off like a bird. First of all the great Tartarin decided to read the accounts of the great African travellers, the journals of Mungo Park, Caillé, Doctor Livingstone and Henri Duveyrier. Here he read, that before strapping on their sandals for distant journeys these brave travellers inured themselves in advance to withstand hunger, thirst, forced marches and privations of all kinds. Tartarin decided to take them as his model and from that very day to feed only on a broth of hot water with a clove of garlic, a sprig of thyme and a bit of bay-leaf. The diet was strict and you can imagine the faces that poor Sancho made.

In addition to this broth diet, Tartarin adopted some other wise precautions. Thus, to acquire the habit of long marches, he forced himself to make his tour of the town seven or eight times every morning without stopping, sometimes at a fast walk, sometimes at a run with his elbows drawn in to his sides and a couple of white pebbles in his mouth, according to the ancient fashion. Then to accustom himself to the night chills, fogs and dews, he went down into his garden each night and stayed there till ten or eleven o'clock, alone with his rifle, on the watch behind the baobab. Finally, so long as the Mitaine menagerie remained at Tarascon, the cap-shooters who had stayed late at Costecalde's would see in the shadows as they crossed the Place du Château, a mysterious man walking up and down behind the tent. It was Tartarin of Tarascon, accustoming himself to hear without trembling the roaring of lions in the darkest night.

Before the Departure

While Tartarin was thus training himself by all sorts of heroic means the whole of Tarascon had its eyes on him; no interest was shown in anything else. Cap-shooting was neglected, and ballad-singing was suspended. At Bézuquet the chemist's the piano languished beneath a green cloth on which Spanish flies dried with their legs aloft. Tartarin's expedition had put a stop to everything. You should have seen the great man's success in the drawing-rooms. They snatched at him, they quarrelled over him, they borrowed him, they stole him from one another. There was no greater honour for the ladies than to visit Mitaine's menagerie on Tartarin's arm and make him explain before the lion's cage how you set about hunting these great beasts, where you had to aim and from how many yards away, whether there were many accidents, etc., etc.

Tartarin furnished all the desired explanations. He had read Jules Gerard and was as conversant with everything about lion-hunting as if he had actually hunted the lion. So he spoke of all these matters with great eloquence. But where he shone brightest was in the evenings, at dinner with President Ladeveze or the brave Major Bravida. When coffee was brought in and all the chairs were pulled close, they would make him talk about his future hunting. Then, with his elbow on the tablecloth and his nose in his coffee our hero would relate in emotional tones all the dangers awaiting him over there. He spoke of long watches for game on moonless nights, of plague-ridden marshes, of rivers poisoned by the leaves of the rose-laurel, of snows and scorching suns, scorpions and showers of locusts; he spoke also of the habits of the great lions of Atlas, their way of fighting, their phenomenal strength, and their fierceness at times of rut. Then, excited by his own tale, he would rise from the table, leap into the middle of the dining-room, imitating the lion's roar, the report of a carbine and the whistle of an explosive bullet. Pftt! Pftt! He gesticulated, he roared, he overturned the chairs.

Around the table everyone turned pale. The gentlemen

exchanged glances and nodded their heads, the ladies shut their eyes and gave little screams of fear, the small boys who were put to bed early, woken with a start by the roars and the gun-fire, cried in terror for a light.

Meanwhile, Tartarin did not start.

Let's fight it out with Swords, Gentlemen! Sword-thrusts not Pinpricks

Did he really intend to set out? A delicate question which Tartarin's historian would be highly embarrassed to answer. The fact is that Mitaine's menagerie had left Tarascon over three months and still the lion-killer did not stir. After all, perhaps our candid hero, blinded by a new mirage, believed in good faith that he had really gone to Algeria. Perhaps, on the strength of having related his future exploits, he imagined that he had performed them as sincerely as he had once imagined that he had run up the consular flag and fired on the Tartars—Bang-bang! at Shanghai.

Unfortunately if Tartarin was this time once more deceived by his own mirage, the people of Tarascon were not. When after three months' waiting they observed that the hunter had not yet packed a single trunk they began to mutter. 'This is going to be another Shanghai!' said Costecalde with a smile, and the gunsmith's remark ran right through the town, for no one believed in Tartarin any more. The simpletons and cowards, men like Bézuquet who would have been frightened by a flea and could not fire a gun without closing their eyes, were particularly merciless. In the club, on the esplanade, they greeted Tartarin with little bantering smiles.

'Tell me, when's this trip coming off?'

In Costecalde's shop Tartarin's opinion was no longer accepted. The cap-shooters disowned their chief. Then witticisms began to be added. President Ladeveze, who in his leisure moments paid some slight court to the Provençal muse, made up a song in the local dialect, which had a great success. It was about a certain great hunter called Master Gervais whose dreaded rifle was said to have exterminated every lion in Africa down to the very last. Unluckily this deadly rifle was of a strange kind: *though it was always being loaded it never went off*. Never went off. You catch the allusion?

In less than no time this song became popular, and when Tartarin passed, the porters on the river-bank and the ragamuffins in front of his door sang out in chorus:

> Master Jarvey's rifle, loaded every minute,
> Master Jarvey's rifle, tons of bullets in it,
> Master Jarvey's rifle's loaded right enough
> But Master Jarvey's rifle never does go off.

But the song was sung from some distance away on account of his muscles, twice normal size. As for the great man, he pretended to see nothing, to hear nothing. But under the surface this stifled and venomous little war grieved him greatly. He felt Tarascon sliding out of his hands, its popular favour going to others, and this made him suffer dreadfully. Popularity is like a great eating-trough. It is nice to have a seat in front of it, but what a scalding you get when it is overturned! Despite his suffering Tartarin smiled and went on peacefully leading his usual life as if there were nothing the matter. Sometimes however this mask of joyful indifference, glued to his face by pride, suddenly slipped. Instead of laughter, grief and indignation came into view. Thus it was one morning when the little ragamuffins were singing under his windows *'Master Jarvey's rifle'*, their voices reached the poor, great man's room just as he was shaving in front of his mirror (Tartarin had a full beard, but as it grew very thick he was obliged to keep it trimmed). Suddenly the window was violently opened and Tartarin appeared in his shirtsleeves and night-cap, smothered in lather and brandishing his razor, soap and brush. 'Sword-thrusts, gentlemen,' he shouted, 'sword-thrusts by all means but not pinpricks.'

Fine words, worthy of history's record. Only one thing was wrong, that they were addressed to little urchins, no taller than their boot-boxes, to gentlemen quite incapable of wielding a sword.

A Dialogue at the House of the Baobab

In the midst of the general defection, only the army stuck out for Tartarin. Brave Major Bravida continued to show him the same esteem. 'He's a sportsman,' repeated the ex-superintendent of the clothing store stubbornly, and this assertion, I believe, was worth as much as Bézuquet the chemist's. The worthy major had never once referred to the trip to Africa. However when the public outcry became very strong he decided to speak.

One evening the unhappy Tartarin was alone in his study

thinking sad thoughts, when he saw the major come in. His expression was grave, he wore black gloves and was buttoned up to the neck.

'Tartarin,' said the superintendent in a voice of command. 'Tartarin. You must go.' He remained standing in the doorway, tall and stern as duty herself. Tartarin understood the full import of those words 'You must go'. He arose very pale and cast a tender eye at his pleasant study all round him, so snug, so full of warmth and soft light, at his large very comfortable easy-chair, at his books, his carpets, the long white blinds of his windows, beyond which quivered the slender branches of his little garden. Then advancing towards the brave major, he took his hand, squeezed it firmly and in a voice that echoed with tears, yet stoical for all that, said: 'I will go, Bravida.'

And he went as he had promised. Only still not immediately. He needed time to equip himself. First of all he ordered from Bompard two large brass-bound gun-cases each with a long plaque bearing the inscription

TARTARIN OF TARASCON   FIREARMS

The binding and the lettering took much time. He also ordered from Tastavin a magnificent traveller's diary in which to write his journal and impressions. For after all though one may be hunting the lion one will still have thoughts on the way. Then he sent to Marseilles for a whole cargo of tinned foods, and pemmican in tablets to make broth, a tent-shelter of a new pattern which could be erected and taken down in a minute, sea-boots, a couple of umbrellas, a water-proof and blue glasses to prevent ophthalmia. Last of all Bézuquet the chemist prepared him a small portable medicine chest stuffed with plasters, arnica, camphor and medicated spirits.

Poor Tartarin, he was not taking all this on his own behalf. But he hoped by dint of precautions and tender attentions to calm the fury of Tartarin-Sancho, who had been in a continuous temper all day and all night ever since the departure had been decided on.

The Departure

Finally the great and solemn day arrived. All Tarascon had been up since dawn, crowding the Avignon road and the approaches to the little house of the baobab. People at the windows, on the roofs, up the trees; Rhône bargees, porters, ragamuffins, shopkeepers, girls from the cloth mills, from the taffeta factory, the club, in fact the whole town; and some people from Beaucaire also who had crossed the bridge, market-gardeners from the outskirts, great tilted carts, vine-dressers on handsome mules decked out with ribbons, streamers, bells, rosettes and rattles. There was even a sprinkling of pretty girls from Arles, their heads tied up with blue ribbons. They had come in behind their young men who rode the steel-grey horses of the Camargue.

This whole crowd was pressing and jostling before Tartarin's door, before the door of that good Monsieur Tartarin who was going off to the 'Turks' to kill lions in Turkey. For the people of Tarascon, Algeria, Africa, Greece, Turkey, Mesopotamia, all formed a very vague, almost mythological country called 'the Turks'.

In the midst of this throng, the cap-shooters came and went, proud of their chief's triumph and leaving trails of glory behind them as they passed.

In front of the house of the baobab stood two large hand-carts. Every now and then, the door opened to give a view of a few persons gravely walking up and down the little garden. Men were carrying trunks, boxes and night bags which were piled on the handcarts. At each new load, the crowd quivered. The articles were named aloud: 'That there is the tent-shelter' . . . 'There is the tinned food' . . . 'That's the medicine chest' . . . 'Those are the gun-cases' . . . And the cap-shooters entered into explanations. Suddenly towards ten o'clock there was a great commotion in the crowd. The garden door swung violently on its hinges. 'Here he is! Here he is!' someone shouted. It was he. When he appeared in the doorway cries of fear rose from the crowd: 'It's a Turk' . . . 'He's wearing spectacles.'

Tartarin of Tarascon had indeed thought it correct since he was going to Algeria to wear Algerian costume: large baggy trousers of white cloth, a little close-fitting jacket with metal buttons, a red sash two foot wide round his stomach, his neck bare and his forehead shaved, on his head a huge red fez or *chechia* with a blue tassel of enormous length. In addition two heavy guns, one on each shoulder, a large hunting-knife in his sash, a cartridge belt around his middle and on his hip a revolver swinging in a leather holster. That is all. But forgive me, I was forgetting the spectacles, an enormous pair of blue spectacles acted as a useful corrective to the over-wild details in our hero's outfit.

'Long live Tartarin! Long live Tartarin!' howled the crowd. The great man smiled, but did not bow on account of the guns which hindered him. Moreover he now knew how much reliance could be put on popular favour. Perhaps even at the bottom of his heart he cursed his terrible compatriots who were forcing him to set out, to leave his pretty little white-walled home with the green shutters. But he gave no sign of this.

Proudly and calmly, although a little pale, he came out into the roadway, looked at his handcarts to see that everything was all right, jauntily took the road to the railway station without glancing back even once at the house of the baobab tree. Behind him marched brave Major Bravida and President Ladeveze, and next Costecalde the gunsmith and all the cap-shooters, after whom came the carts and then the crowd. In front of the booking-hall the station master awaited him, an African veteran of the 1830 campaign, who shook Tartarin's hand with fervour again and again. The Paris–Marseilles express had not yet come in. Tartarin and his staff went into the waiting-rooms to avoid congestion, the station master had the barrier closed behind them. For a quarter of an hour Tartarin walked up and down these rooms, surrounded by the cap-shooters. He talked to them about his journey and about hunting, and promised to send them some skins. Names were entered for skins in his note-book as for dances on a dance-card.

Calm and quiet, like Socrates at the moment of swallowing the hemlock, the bold Tartarin had a word for each one, a smile for everybody. He spoke simply and in affable tones; it was as if on departing he wished to leave a train of charm, regrets and pleasant memories behind him. Tears started to the cap-shooters' eyes as they listened to their chief's gentle words. Some of them, like President Ladeveze and Bézuquet, even felt remorse. Some of the station staff were weeping in corners. Outside, the crowd was looking through the bars and shouting, 'Long live Tartarin!'

At last the bell rang. A dull rumbling was heard and a whistle that shook the roof. 'All aboard! All aboard!'

'Good-bye, Tartarin! Good-bye, Tartarin.'

'Good-bye to you all!' murmured the great man, and in the person of the worthy Major Bravida he embraced his beloved Tarascon. Then he leapt on to the track and got into a carriage full of Parisian ladies, who thought they would die of terror at the sight of this strange man with all his pistols and rifles coming in to join them.

The Port of Marseilles. All aboard! All aboard!

On December 1, 186.., at midday under a wintry Provençal sun, in clear, brilliant and splendid weather the astonished inhabitants of Marseilles saw a *Turk*, a real Turk walk out on to the Canebière. They had never seen anything like him, and yet heaven knows there's no shortage of Turks at Marseilles. The Turk in question—is it needful to say?—was Tartarin, the great Tartarin of Tarascon walking along the quays followed by his gun-cases, his medicine chest and his tins of food, to reach the landing-stage of Compagnie Touache and the mail steamer *Zouave* which was to take him overseas.

His ears still ringing with Tarascon's cheers, intoxicated by the light in the sky and the smell of the sea, Tartarin marched joyfully with his guns on his shoulder and his head high, gazing with all attention on that marvellous port of Marseilles, which he was seeing for the first time. It dazzled him. The poor man believed he was dreaming. He imagined his name was Sinbad the Sailor and that he was wandering in one of those fantastic cities that he had read of in *The Arabian Nights*.

There was a forest of masts stretching as far as the eye could see, of spars pointing in all directions. Flags of every nation, Russian, Greek, Swedish, Tunisian, American. The ships on a level with the wharves, the bowsprits sticking up above the mole like rows of bayonets, and beneath them naiads, goddesses, holy virgins and other painted wooden figureheads, denoting the names of the ships: all this rotten with sea-water, eaten away, dripping and sodden. Here and there between the ships was a patch of sea like a big piece of watered silk splashed with oil. Framed by the masts and spars were crowds of sea-gulls which made a pleasant pattern against the blue sky, and there were also cabin-boys calling to one another in every language. On the quay among the thick green or brackish streams bringing down oil and scum from the soap-works, stood a crowd of customs officers, messengers, porters with their *bogies* drawn by small Corsican ponies. Shops selling strange objects, smoky booths in which sailors were doing their cooking, sellers of pipes, sellers of monkeys, parrots, rope, sail-cloth, fantastic bric-à-brac among which old culverins, great gilded lanterns, old pulley-blocks, old flukeless anchors, old rope, shouting-horns and marine glasses from the time of the old captains, were laid out higgledy-piggledy. Sellers of mussels and shrimps called their wares as they squatted beside them.

Sailors passed with pots of tar, smoking stew-pots, or great baskets full of cuttlefish that they were going to wash in the whitish water of the fountains. Everywhere prodigious piles of goods of all sorts: silks, minerals, stacks of timber, pigs of lead, cloth, sugar, carob-beans, colza seed, liquorice root, sugar-canes, the East and West all mixed up. Great piles of Dutch cheeses that the Genoese dye red by hand.

Over there was the grain quay; stevedores were discharging their sacks on the top of high shoots on the mole. Golden torrents of wheat rolled down, raising a yellow dust. Men in red fezes were sifting it in large donkey-leather sieves and loading it on carts which went off followed by a regiment of women and children with brushes and gleaning baskets. Further off was the dock, in which great vessels lay on their sides, their yards dipping in the water, while their timbers were scorched with brushwood to remove the seaweed. There was a smell of pitch, and the deafening sound of the sheathers lining the ships' sides with great plates of copper. Sometimes there was a gap between the masts. Then Tartarin saw the entrance to the harbour, the great coming and going of ships, a smart, well-scoured English frigate setting sail for Malta with its officers in yellow gloves, or a home-port brig perhaps hauling out to the accompaniment of much shouting and swearing, with a fat captain in a frock-coat and silk hat standing in the bows and controlling operations in the local dialect. Ships were departing swiftly with all sails set. Others further off were coming up slowly in the sunshine, and seemed to be suspended in the air.

And all the time there was a frightful din, the rumbling of the carts, the 'Haul away!' of the sailors, oaths, singing, the steamers' sirens, the drums and bugles of Fort Saint-Jean and Fort Saint-Nicholas, and the bells of La Major, Les Accoules and Saint Victor. On top of it all the mistral caught up the clatter and clamour and rolled them and shook them and mingled them with its own voice. It made a wild, crazy and heroic music, like a great fanfare of farewell, a fanfare which made a man long to depart, to have wings and go on a far journey. It was to the sound of this grand fanfare that the bold Tartarin of Tarascon embarked for the country of the lions.

Second Episode

In the Land of the Turks

The Crossing. The five Positions of the Fez. The Evening of the third Day. Lord have Mercy!

I wish I were a painter, dear readers, and a good one, so that I could show you at the head of this second episode the different positions assumed by Tartarin of Tarascon's fez during his three-day crossing aboard the *Zouave* from France to Algeria. I would show it to you first of all on deck as they set out, all proud and heroic, like a halo of glory around his fine Tarasconian head. I would show it to you next as they left the harbour and the *Zouave* began to sport upon the breakers; I would show it trembling with astonishment and as if already feeling the first qualms of sickness. Then, on the Gulf of Lyons, as they advanced into the open sea and the waves became rougher, I would depict it wrestling with the storm, and standing fearfully on our hero's skull with its great blue woollen tassel bristling in the sea-mist and spray. Fourth position at six in the evening, within sight of the Corsican coast. The unfortunate fez is hanging over the ship's rail, and lamentably staring down to measure the depth of the sea. Finally, the fifth and last position, at the end of a narrow cabin, in a little bunk that looked like the drawer of a dressing chest, a wretched and shapeless object rolling and groaning on the pillow. This was the fez, so heroic as the ship steamed out but now reduced to a common night-cap, pulled down on the head of a pallid and heaving sufferer.

Oh, if the citizens of Tarascon could have seen their great

Tartarin lying in his chest drawer under the sad, thin light that seeped through the port-holes, amid the stale smell of cooking and wet timber, the depressing odour of steamships; if they could have heard him gasping at each turn of the screw and calling for tea every five minutes, and cursing the ship's boy in a thin, piping voice, they would have reproached themselves for ever having compelled him to set out. Believe me who tell the story, the unfortunate Turk was a pitiful sight. Suddenly smitten with sea-sickness, the poor man had not had the strength to undo his Algerian sash, or to rid himself of his arsenal. His great-handled hunting-knife was bruising his chest, his leather revolver holster was thumping his thigh. And to crown everything came the taunts of Tartarin-Sancho whose groans and abuse were unceasing:

'What an imbecile! Didn't I tell you. You would go to Africa! Well, here's Africa in front of you. How do you like it?'

The cruellest thing of all was that from the depths of his cabin and in the intervals between his groans, the poor man could hear the passengers in the great saloon laughing, eating, singing and playing cards. Society on the *Zouave* was both cheerful and numerous. It consisted of officers rejoining their regiments, ladies from the Alcazar music-hall in Marseilles, a touring company, a rich Muslim on his way back from Mecca, a Montenegrin prince who was a great wag and gave imitations of all the best Paris comedians. Not one of these people was sea-sick; they spent their time drinking champagne with the captain of the *Zouave*, a stout liver of the gay life who had a family at Marseilles and another at Algiers, and answered to the jolly name of

Barbassou. Tartarin of Tarascon hated this whole wretched crowd. Their cheerfulness made him even more seasick.

Finally on the afternoon of the third day, there was an unaccustomed stir aboard which roused our hero from his long stupor. The forward bell sounded. Heavy seaman's boots could be heard running on the deck.

'Ahead now,' cried the hoarse voice of Captain Barbassou. 'Now astern.' Then, 'Stop her dead!' There was sudden shock. All movement stopped, and nothing more. Nothing but the steamship rolling quietly to right and left, like a balloon in the air.

This strange silence alarmed Tartarin. 'Lord have mercy on us, we're sinking!' he cried in a voice of terror. Miraculously recovering his strength, he leapt from his bunk and rushed on to the deck with his arsenal.

To Arms! To Arms!

They were not sinking, they had arrived. The *Zouave* had just entered the roads, a fine anchorage with black deep water, but silent, mournful and almost deserted. Facing them, on a hill, was the white city of Algiers with its little dead white houses crowded close together and dropping down to the sea. It looked like washing day on Meudon hill. Overhead was wide blue satin sky. Oh, what a blue!

Slightly recovered from his fright the illustrious Tartarin looked at the view, listening respectfully to the Montenegrin prince who stood beside him naming the different quarters of the city, the Casbah, the upper city, the Rue Bab-Azoun.

This Montenegrin prince was very well-bred. What was more, he knew Algeria inside out and spoke fluent Arabic. So Tartarin decided to cultivate his acquaintance. Suddenly, along the rail against which they were leaning, the Tarasconian saw a line of large black hands clinging to it from the other side . . . Almost instantly a negro's woolly head appeared in front of him, and before he had time to open his mouth the deck was invaded from all sides by a hundred black or yellow pirates, hideous, terrifying and half naked. These pirates, Tartarin knew . . . were *them*. That is to say They, the famous THEY that he had so often looked for at night in the streets of Tarascon. So they had decided to come at last.

At first surprise riveted him to the spot. But when he saw the ruffians leap upon the baggage, tear off the tarpaulin that covered it and then begin to pillage the ship, our hero awoke. Whipping out his hunting-knife, he cried 'To arms! To arms!' to the other passengers, and in advance of them all fell on the pirates.

'What's all this? What's the matter? What's gone wrong with you?' cried Captain Barbassou, coming up from between decks.

'Ah, here you are, Captain! Quick, quick! Arm your men.'

'Eh? What for, in God's name?'

'But can't you see?'

'See what?'

'There in front of you. Pirates.'

Captain Barbassou looked at him in astonishment. At this moment a great devil of a negro ran past them with our hero's medicine chest on his back.

'Here, you wretch! Wait for me,' yelled the Tarasconian

and rushed forward with his knife. Barbassou caught him on the wing, and held him by his sash.

'Keep quiet, won't you, for God's sake. They're not pirates. There have been no pirates for donkeys' years. These men are baggage-porters.'

'Eh? Porters?'

'Yes, porters. They've come to fetch the baggage and take it ashore. Put that cutlass away. Give me your ticket and follow that negro. He's a good lad. He'll take you ashore, and to your hotel too, if you want him to . . .'

Slightly abashed, Tartarin handed over his ticket, and went after the negro. He climbed down the rope ladder into a large boat which danced alongside. His luggage was already there, his trunks, his gun-cases and tinned food, and as they filled the whole boat there was no need to wait for other passengers. The negro climbed on to the trunks and squatted like a monkey, clasping his knees. Another negro took the oars. Both laughed as they looked at Tartarin, and showed their white teeth. Standing in the bows, with that terrible grimace which struck terror into his fellow-citizens, the great Tarasconian feverishly clutched the handle of his knife. For despite what Barbassou had said, he was only half reassured concerning the intentions of these ebony-skinned porters, who bore so little resemblance to the good porters of Tarascon.

Five minutes later the boat came to land and Tartarin set foot on that little Barbary quay where three hundred years before a Spanish galley-slave called Miguel Cervantes, beneath the cane of an Algerian overseer, was devising a sublime romance the name of which was to be *Don Quixote*.

Invocation to Cervantes. Landing. Where are the Turks? There are no Turks. Disillusionment

O Miguel Cervantes Saavedra, if what they say is true and in the places where great men have lived some traces of them still remain hovering in the air till the end of time, what remained of you on the Barbary coast must have leapt with joy on seeing Tartarin of Tarascon come ashore. For in that marvellous type of Southern Frenchman the two heroes of your book Don Quixote and Sancho Panza were embodied.

The air was sultry that day. On the quay which was bathed in sunshine were five or six customs officers. Algerians waiting for news from France, a few Moors squatting and smoking their long pipes, some Maltese sailors dragging in large nets in the mesh of which thousands of sardines glittered like little silver coins. But no sooner did Tartarin step ashore than the quay sprang into life and changed its appearance. A horde of savages still more hideous than the pirates on the boat got up from among the pebbles of the shore and rushed on the new arrival. Tall Arabs completely naked beneath their woollen blankets, little Moors in rags, negroes, Tunisians, Minorcans, M'zabites from the Sahara, hotel waiters in white aprons, all shrieking and shouting and clutching at his clothes, and quarrelling over his luggage. One seized his tinned food, another his medicine chest and all in an impossible gibberish hurled the names of improbable hotels in his face.

Bewildered by all this tumult, poor Tartarin walked hither and thither, swore, cursed, lost his head and ran after his luggage. Not knowing how to make himself understood by these barbarians, he harangued them in French, in Provençal and even in Latin, the Latin of the primer, *rosa a rose*, *bonus*, *bona*, *bonum*, which was as much as he knew. He was wasting his pains. No one listened. Fortunately a little man in a tunic with a yellow collar intervened like a god in Homer. Armed with a long cane he plunged into the crowd and dispersed all this riff-raff with a rain of blows. He was an Algerian policeman. Very politely, he persuaded Tartarin to put up at the Hotel de l'Europe, placed him in the care of some local porters who escorted him there after loading his baggage on several barrows.

As he took his first walk in Algiers, Tartarin of Tarascon boggled with surprise. He had imagined a fantastic city, part myth, part fairy-tale, something halfway between Constantinople and Zanzibar. But it was exactly like Tarascon. Cafés, restaurants, wide streets, four-storeyed houses, and a little paved square in which an infantry band was playing Offenbach polkas and gentlemen were sitting on café chairs drinking beer and eating snacks. There were some ladies too, a few tarts, and some soldiers . . . but not a *Turk*! He was the only one, and he felt rather awkward as he crossed the square. Everybody looked at him, the infantry band stopped, leaving their Offenbach polka with one leg in the air.

With his two guns on his shoulders and his revolver at his hip, like a wild and majestic Robinson Crusoe, Tartarin walked gravely between these various groups. But when he reached the hotel his strength deserted him. His mind was in confusion. The departure from Tarascon, the port of Marseilles, the crossing, the Montenegrin prince, the pirates, were spinning through his head. He had to be taken up to his room, disarmed and undressed. At first they talked of sending for a doctor. But the moment his head touched the pillow our hero began to snore loud and heartily. The landlord concluded therefore that no aid from science was necessary, and everyone discreetly withdrew.

The first Watch for Game

Three o'clock was striking on the Government House clock when Tartarin awoke. He had slept right through the evening and night and the next morning and a good part of the afternoon. It must be added that in the last three days his fez had had some rough shocks. The hero's first thought on opening his eyes was this, 'Here I am in the country of the lions.' But why not say here and now: at the idea that the lions were quite near, only a couple of yards away, and that he would have to face up to them. Brr! a deathly shiver ran through him and he boldly dived under the bedclothes.

But after a few minutes, the gaiety outside, the blue sky, the bright sun streaming into his room, a good breakfast which he had served him in bed, his window which opened wide on the sea—all these washed down by an excellent bottle of Corsican wine quickly restored his old heroic spirit. 'Now for the lions!' he cried as he threw off the bedclothes and briskly dressed himself.

This was his plan: to leave the city without saying a word

to anyone, to go straight out into the desert and wait for night. Then he would lie in ambush and Bang, bang! at the first lion that came by. Next day he would come back to breakfast at the Hotel de l'Europe and receive the congratulations of the natives. Then he would hire a cart to go out and fetch his lion.

He hurriedly armed himself therefore and coiled his tent-shelter on his back. Its stout centre-post stuck up a good foot above his head, as stiff as a ramrod, when he came down into the street. Not wanting to ask anyone the way for fear of revealing his purpose, he turned resolutely to the right and threaded the Bab-Azoun arcades to the end. Here swarms of Algerian Jews, lying in ambush like spiders, in the dark corners of their shops, watched him pass.

He crossed the Place du Théâtre, followed the Faubourg and finally the great dusty Mustapha highway. On this road there was a fantastic conglomeration of omnibuses, cabs, two-wheeled carriages, army wagons, great haycarts drawn by oxen, squads of Chasseurs d'Afrique, droves of microscopic donkeys, negresses selling biscuits, Alsatian emigrants' carts, Spahis in scarlet cloaks, all passing in a cloud of dust to the sound of shouting, singing and military bugles. On both sides of the road was a line of vile hovels, drinking-shops full of soldiers, butchers' and knackers' booths, and others where lanky whores could be seen combing their hair at the doors.

'What nonsense they talked to me about the East,' thought the great Tartarin. 'There are not as many Turks here as at Marseilles.'

Suddenly he saw a magnificent camel strut past like a turkey stretching its long legs. This set his heart beating.

Camels already! Lions could not be far off now. Five minutes later he saw a company of lion-hunters approaching with their rifles on their backs. 'Cowards,' thought our hero as they came level with him. 'Cowards to be hunting lions in companies and with dogs!' For it had never occurred to him that in Algeria people could hunt anything but lions. But these hunters had the kindly faces of retired shopkeepers, and this way of hunting the lion with dogs and game-bags was so patriarchal that the Tarasconian, slightly perplexed, thought he should approach one of these gentlemen.

'Tell me now, friend, have you had good sport?'

'Not bad,' replied the hunter, taking a frightened look at the Tarasconian warrior's ample armaments.

'Had a kill?'

'Oh yes . . . Not a bad haul. Take a look.' And the Algerian hunter displayed his game-bag bulging with rabbits and woodcock.

'What? In your game-bag? You put them in your game-bag?'

'Where do you expect me to put them?'

'But I say . . . they must be very small ones.'

'Some small and some big as well,' answered the sportsman. And as he was in a hurry to get home he strode out to rejoin his comrades.

The bold Tartarin stopped in the middle of the road, transfixed with bewilderment. Then after a moment's reflexion, he said to himself: 'Bah, they're a bunch of jokers. They haven't had a kill at all . . .' And he continued on his way.

Already the houses were getting fewer, and passers-by also. Night was falling, and things were getting indistinct.

Tartarin of Tarascon walked on for another half-hour, after which he stopped. It was now quite dark. A moonless night, sprinkled with stars. No one on the road. But after all, our hero thought, lions are not stage-coaches. They would not willingly travel on the main road. So he plunged into the fields. There were ditches, brambles and bushes at every step. No matter. He went on walking. Then suddenly he stopped.

'There's a scent of lions round here,' said our friend, and gave a good sniff to left and right.

Bang! bang!

It was a great wild desert, bristling with strange plants, with those Eastern plants that look like savage beasts. In the faint starlight their long shadows extended across the ground in all directions. On the right loomed the heavy mass of a mountain, perhaps the Atlas. On the left the dull tossing of the invisible sea. The real place to attract big game. With one rifle in front of him and another in his hands, Tartarin put a knee to the ground and waited. He waited for an hour, for two hours. Nothing!

Then he remembered that the great lion-killers in his books never went hunting without taking a kid. They tethered it some yards in front of them, and made it bleat by tugging its paw with a string. Having no kid, the Tarasconian thought of trying some imitations, and started bleating in a goatlike voice: first very softly because in the bottom of his heart he was still somewhat afraid that the lion might hear him. But since nothing came he bleated more loudly: 'Me-e, me-e!' Still nothing. Losing patience, he began again even louder and several times in succession, 'Me-e, me-e, me-e,' with such power that his kid began to sound like a bull.

Suddenly something very large and black came down some yards in front of him. He went quiet. The thing lowered its head and sniffed the ground, bounded up, rolled over, galloped off, came back and stopped dead. Now it was easy to distinguish its four short legs, its massive neck, and its eyes, two large eyes that gleamed in the dark. Up went Tartarin's gun. He fired, Bang, bang! It was over. Then a sudden leap backwards, and the drawing of a hunting-knife. The Tarasconian's shot was answered by a terrible howl.

'He's got it,' cried the good Tartarin, and steadying himself on his strong legs, he prepared to receive the beast's charge. But it had had more than enough and ran away at top speed still howling. He did not stir however. He was expecting its mate to come . . . as she does in all the books. But unfortunately the female did not come. After waiting two or three hours, the Tarasconian grew weary. The earth was damp, the night was getting cold, the sea wind stung him.

'I've a good mind to take a nap till daybreak,' he said to himself, and turned to his tent-shelter to protect him from rheumatism. But the devil of it was that the tent-shelter was of a most ingenious construction, so ingenious in fact that he could not manage to open it. He sweated and fenced with it for a whole hour but in vain; the confounded tent did not open. There are umbrellas which delight in playing you this sort of trick in torrential downpours. Weary of the struggle, the Tarasconian threw the contraption down and lay on it, swearing like the true Provençal he was.

'Ta, ta, ra, ta, tarata!'

'What's that?' exclaimed Tartarin, waking with a start.

It was the bugles of the Chasseurs d'Afrique sounding the Reveille in the Mustapha barracks. The lion-hunter rubbed his eyes in bewilderment. And he had thought he was in the desert! Do you know where he was? In an artichoke field, between a patch of cauliflowers and another of beetroot. His Sahara grew vegetables.

Close to him, on the pretty green slope of Upper Mustapha, Algerian villas, white all over, were glistening with the dew beneath the rising sun; anybody might think he was in the neighbourhood of Marseilles, among all the little country houses. The middle-class vegetable-garden appearance of this sleeping landscape greatly surprised the poor man and put him in a very bad temper. 'These people are mad,' he said to himself, 'to plant their artichokes in lion country. For after all, I wasn't dreaming. Lions do come as far as here, and there's the proof.' The proof was the stains of blood that the beast had left in its flight. Bending over this red trail, with watchful eye and his hand on his revolver the brave Tarasconian advanced from artichoke to artichoke as far as a little field of oats. Trampled grass, a pool of blood, and in the middle of the pool, lying on its side with a large wound in its head, a . . . Guess what!

A lion, of course.

No, a donkey, one of those little donkeys that are so common in Algeria, where they're generally called *Neddy*.

Arrival of the Female. Terrible Combat. The Sportsmen's Retreat

Tartarin's first feeling at the sight of his wretched victim was one of pity. There is such a wide difference between a lion and a poor moke. His second feeling was one of pity also. The poor moke was so pretty, and looked such a nice animal. The hide on his still warm flanks heaved and fell like the waves. Tartarin knelt down and tried to stanch the poor creature's blood with the end of his Algerian sash. You cannot imagine a more touching sight, than this great man dressing the little donkey's wound. At the touch of the silken sash the donkey, who had scarcely a ha'porth of life in him, opened his large grey eye, and twitched his long ears two or three times as if to say, 'Thank you, thank you.' Then a final convulsion shook him from head to tail and he did not stir again.

'Blacky! Blacky!' suddenly cried a voice choking with anguish. At the same time the branches quivered in a nearby thicket. Tartarin had only just time to stand up and place himself on guard. It was the female.

She approached roaring terribly in the person of an old Alsatian woman with her head tied up in a kerchief, and armed with a large red umbrella. She was crying for her donkey till all Mustapha rang with the echoes. It would have been better for Tartarin to have had a furious lioness to deal with than this ugly old woman. In vain the poor man tried to make her understand how the accident had happened, and that he had taken Blacky for a lion. The old woman thought that she was being made fun of and with strenuous cries of 'Der Teufel!' she fell on our hero, beating him with her umbrella. Tartarin, in some confusion, defended himself as best he could. He parried her blows with his carbine, puffing, sweating, leaping and crying: 'But Madame . . . Madame.'

To no purpose. Madame was deaf, as her blows proved. Fortunately a third person arrived on the battlefield, the Alsatian woman's husband. He was Alsatian too, an inn-keeper and, what was more, a good calculator. When he realized what kind of customer he had to deal with, and that the killer was perfectly willing to pay the fair value of his victim, he disarmed his spouse and an agreement was reached.

Tartarin gave him two hundred francs, the donkey being worth about ten. At least, this was the current price of mokes in the Arab markets. Then they buried poor Blacky at the foot of a fig-tree, and the Alsatian, put into a good mood by the colour of the Tarasconian cash, invited our hero to come and break a crust at his inn, which lay some yards away beside the main road. Algerian sportsmen came to lunch there on Sundays, for the plain was full of game, and it was the best place for rabbit-shooting anywhere near the city.

'What about lions?' asked Tartarin.

The Alsatian looked at him in great astonishment. 'Lions?'

'Yes, lions. Don't you see them sometimes?' pursued the poor man with rather less assurance.

The inn-keeper burst out laughing.

'God bless my soul! Lions? What would we do with lions?'

'Aren't there any in Algeria then?'

'I've never seen one, I promise you, and I've lived in this province twenty years. But I believe I've heard stories about them. I think in the newspapers. But that would be a long way from here, down in the South, you know.'

At this point they reached the inn, a suburban inn that might have been Vauvres or Pantin. There was a withered green vine over the door, and billiard cues painted on the walls. Above it was the harmless sign

THE SPORTSMEN'S RETREAT

Sportsmen's retreat, it reminded him of Bravida.

The Story of an Omnibus. A Moorish Lady and a Wreath of Jasmine

This first adventure would have been enough to discourage many. But men of Tartarin's mettle do not allow themselves to be easily cast down. 'The lions are in the South,' thought our hero. 'Very well, I'll go south.' And as soon as he had swallowed his last mouthful, he got up, thanked his host, shed a final tear for the unfortunate Blacky, and returned in great haste to Algiers with the intention of strapping up his luggage and leaving that same day for the South.

Unfortunately, the Mustapha highroad seemed to have grown longer since last night. It was very hot and very dusty, and the tent-shelter was extremely heavy. Tartarin did not feel strong enough to walk to town. He signalled the first omnibus that passed and climbed in. Oh, poor

Tartarin of Tarascon! How much better it would have been for his fame and reputation not to have got into that old bone-shaker but to have continued his way on foot at the risk of being stifled by the weight of the atmosphere, his tent-shelter and his heavy double-barrelled guns.

When Tartarin entered, the bus was full. Right at the end, with his nose in his breviary, was a priest from Algiers with a long black beard. Opposite was a young Moorish merchant smoking strong cigarettes. Then a Maltese sailor and four or five Moorish women with their faces muffled in white linen, so that only their eyes showed. These ladies had just been saying a prayer at the Abd-el-Kader cemetery, but the sight of the graves did not seem to have depressed them. They could be heard giggling and chattering behind their veils and at the same time munching cakes.

Tartarin thought he detected them looking at him a great deal. One in particular, who was sitting opposite him, had fixed her eyes firmly on his and did not shift her gaze for the whole of the journey. Although the lady was veiled, the sparkle in her dark eyes which were lengthened with k'hol, a fine, slender wrist overloaded with gold bracelets which could be glimpsed every now and then between the veils, also the sound of her voice, the graceful, almost child-like movements of her head, told him that beneath that veil was a young, pretty, adorable creature. The unlucky Tartarin did not know how to escape. The mute caress of those lovely Eastern eyes troubled and perturbed him. They tortured him. He went hot and cold.

To finish him off, the lady's slipper joined in; he felt that little slipper moving rapidly over his stout hunting-boots; that dainty slipper running and frisking like a little red mouse. What could he do? Answer that look, that pressure? Yes, but what would be the consequence? But an Eastern love-affair is a very dangerous thing. And in his romantic, Southerner's imagination, the good man saw himself already seized by eunuchs, beheaded, and in addition, sewn up in a leather sack and tossed by the waves with his head beside him. This cooled him a bit. Meanwhile the little slipper continued its exercise and the eyes opposite opened even wider, staring into his, like two black velvet flowers, which seemed to say: 'Pick us.'

The bus stopped. They had reached the Place du Théâtre, where the Rue Bab-Azoun enters it. One by one, swathed in their voluminous trousers and hugging their veils around them, the Moorish ladies got out. Tartarin's neighbour was the last to get up; and as she did so her face came so near to our hero's that her breath brushed his cheek; it had the true scent of youth, jasmine, musk—and cakes.

The Tarasconian resisted no longer. Intoxicated with love and ready for anything, he rushed out behind the fair Moor. At the sound of his clattering equipment, she turned round, put a finger to her veiled mouth, as if to say 'Hush', and suddenly with the other hand threw him a little perfumed wreath of jasmine flowers. Tartarin of Tarascon leant down to pick it up; but as our hero was rather clumsy and heavily loaded with armaments, the operation took some time.

When he straightened up, with the jasmine wreath to his heart, the Moorish beauty had vanished.

Lions of the Atlas, sleep in Peace!

Lions of the Atlas, sleep well. Sleep in peace in your deep lairs, among the aloes and the savage cacti. You have still several days before Tartarin of Tarascon comes to slaughter you. At the moment all his warlike paraphernalia—his gun-cases, medicine chest, tent-shelter, tinned foods—are lying peaceably packed at the Hotel de l'Europe in a corner of Room 36.

Sleep without fear, you great tawny lions. The Tarasconian is searching for his Moorish beauty. Ever since the adventure of the omnibus, the poor man seems to feel the perpetual friskings of that little red mouse on his foot, his huge hunter's foot; and the sea breeze brushing his lips is for ever scented—whatever he may do—with a lovesick odour of sweet cakes and aniseed.

He must have his African beauty. But this is no simple matter. To find once more in a city of a hundred thousand souls someone whom one knows only by her breath, her slippers and the colour of her eyes. Only a Tarasconian, pierced by the dart of love, would be capable of attempting such an undertaking.

The terrible thing is that swathed in their great white veils, all Moorish women are alike. Besides, they go out very little, and if one wants to see them one must climb up to the upper town, the Arab town, the city of the Turks. This upper town is a regular den of cut-throats. Little dark, very narrow streets, ascending steeply between two lines of mysterious houses, whose roofs meet to form a tunnel. Low doorways, very small sad and silent windows, well barred.

And then, to right and left, a warren of very dark stalls, full of ferocious Turks, who look like pirates. Their teeth and whites of their eyes glisten, as they smoke their long pipes and talk in low tones as if planning deeds of violence.

It would be untrue to say that Tartarin walked fearlessly through this frightening city. He was on the contrary much perturbed. In those dark alleys, which his ample form filled from side to side, the good man advanced only with the greatest precautions, with his eyes skinned and his finger on the trigger of his revolver, in the same way as he had walked to the club in Tarascon. Every moment he expected a gang of eunuchs and janissaries to attack him from behind. But the longing to see his lady again gave him the strength and boldness of a giant.

For a whole week the bold Tartarin haunted the upper town. Sometimes he could be seen standing on one leg in front of the Turkish baths waiting for the hour when the ladies come out in crowds, shivering and still smelling of the bath. Sometimes he could be seen crouching at the doors of mosques, panting and sweating as he removed his large boots before entering the holy place.

Occasionally, at nightfall, as he returned heartbroken at having discovered nothing either at the baths or the mosque, Tartarin would hear music coming from the Moorish houses he passed. There was a monotonous singing, the muffled notes of a guitar, the thumping of a tambourine and short female laughs which set his heart pounding.

'Perhaps she is there,' he would say to himself.

Then if the road was deserted, he would go up to one of these houses, lift the heavy knocker of the postern gate and timidly rap. Immediately the singing and laughter stopped.

All that could be heard inside the walls was little vague whisperings, as from a sleeping aviary.

'Let's hang on a bit,' thought our hero. 'Something is going to happen.' What most often happened was a great jar of cold water on his head, or some orange skins and prickly pears. Never anything more serious.

But the lions of Atlas could sleep in peace.

Prince Gregory of Montenegro

For fully a fortnight the unfortunate Tartarin looked for his Algerian lady, and very probably he would have been looking for her still if lovers' luck had not come to his aid in the person of a Montenegrin nobleman. This is how it happened:

Every Saturday night in winter the Grand Theatre of Algiers gives a masked ball, just like the opera in Paris. It is the usual tasteless masked ball of the provincial town. Not many people on the floor, a few Parisians strayed from Buller's or the Casino, foolish virgins following the army, faded men of fashion, carnival figures in decay, five or six little laundresses from Minorca who have taken to the life but still have a vague smell of garlic and saffron sauce surviving from the days of their virtue. The real spectacle is not here but in the foyer transformed for the occasion into a gambling-room. A feverish and motley crowd jostle one another around the long green tablecloths. Turcos on leave staking the few coppers of their pay, Moorish shopkeepers from the upper town, negroes, Maltese, settlers from the interior who have travelled more than a hundred miles to risk the value of a plough or a pair of oxen on a single ace. Pale, trembling and with gritted teeth, they all have that strange uneasy sidelong look of the true gambler, who seems to squint from looking fixedly always at the same card.

A little apart are tribes of Algerian Jews. The whole family come to play. The men wear Eastern dress with the hideous variation of blue stockings and velvet caps. The women are flabby and white-faced and sit very stiffly in their tight gold bodices. Clustered round the table, the whole tribe squeal, plan their game, count on their fingers and make small bets. Only from time to time, after long consultations, a patriarch with the beard of God the Father draws aside and goes to risk the family five-franc piece. Then, for so long as the game lasts, the Hebrews' glittering eyes are turned to the table, terrible dark magnetic eyes that make the gold coins tremble on the cloth and finally draw them softly away as if on a thread.

Then there is argument, quarrelling and oaths of every country, wild shouts in all languages, knives unsheathed, entries of the police and missing money. Into the middle of this saturnalia the great Tartarin strayed one evening in search of forgetfulness and peace of heart. Our hero was wandering alone among the crowd, thinking of his Moorish beauty when amidst the uproar and the chink of coins two or three angry voices were raised at one of the gambling-tables:

'I tell you, sir, that I am twenty francs short!'

'Sir!'

'Well, what, sir?'

'Do you know whom you are speaking to, sir?'

'I should certainly like to know, sir.'

'I am Prince Gregory of Montenegro, sir.'

Much excited by hearing that name, Tartarin pushed his way through the crowd and took up his position in the front rank, proud and happy to find his prince again, that very well-bred Montenegrin prince whose acquaintance he had first made aboard the mail-boat. Unfortunately this noble title, which had so dazzled the good Tarasconian, did not make the slightest impression on the Chasseur officer with whom the Prince was disputing.

'That doesn't tell me much,' said the officer with a sneer. Then turning towards the bystanders: 'Gregory of Montenegro? Anybody know the fellow? Nobody!'

Tartarin, indignant, took a step forward.

'Excuse me. I know the Pri-ince,' he said in a very firm voice, and in his best Tarasconian accent.

The Chasseur officer looked him in the face for a moment, then shrugged his shoulders.

'That's fine, then . . . You two can share the missing twenty francs, and let's hear no more about it.'

Thereupon he turned his back and disappeared into the crowd. The furious Tartarin wanted to rush after him, but the Prince prevented him.

'Don't worry. I'll look after this.'

And taking the Tarasconian by the arm, the Prince drew him quickly outside. . . . When they were in the square Prince Gregory of Montenegro raised his hat, gave our hero his hand and, vaguely remembering his name, began in vibrant tones:

'Monsieur Barbarin.'

'Tartarin,' whispered the other timidly.

'Tartarin, Barbarin, what's it matter? We stand together now in a league of life and death.' And the noble Montenegrin shook Tartarin's hand with fierce energy. You may well suppose that the Tarasconian was proud.

'Pri-ince, Pri-ince,' he repeated, intoxicated.

A quarter of an hour later these two gentlemen were sitting in the Restaurant des Platanes, a pleasant supper-house with terraces built out over the sea. Tucking into a good Russian salad washed down with a pleasant Corsican wine, they renewed acquaintance.

You can imagine no one more attractive than this Montenegrin prince. Thin, slightly built, with crisp hair curled by the tongs, shaved as smooth as if with pumice, his breast starry with strange orders, he had a wily eye, ingratiating manners, and a vaguely Italian accent that made him seem like a Mazarin without moustaches. Deeply versed in the Latin tongues, he would quote Tacitus, Horace and Caesar's Commentaries upon the slightest excuse.

He was of an old noble family, and his brother had apparently sent him into exile at the age of ten on account of his liberal opinions. Since then he had been wandering the world for instruction and pleasure, in the character of the philosopher prince. By a remarkable coincidence he had spent three years at Tarascon; and when Tartarin expressed amazement at never having met him at the club or on the Esplanade, His Highness observed evasively: 'I went out very little.' The Tarasconian, out of delicacy, ventured no further questions. All great existences have their mysterious aspects.

Prince Gregory was a kind gentleman at heart, and as he sipped his Corsican rosé he listened patiently while Tartarin spoke of his Moorish beauty. He even promised that, knowing all these ladies, he would find her in a very short time. They drank hard and for a long time, toasting 'the ladies of Algiers' and 'a free Montenegro'. Outside, the sea rolled in the darkness and the waves beat beneath the terrace with the sound of wet sheets flapping. The air was warm, and the sky was full of stars. The nightingale sang in the plane-tree. And it was Tartarin who paid the bill.

Tell me your Father's Name and I'll tell you the Name of this Flower

Nothing like a Montenegrin prince for cunningly flushing the birds. At daybreak on the morning after their party at the Platanes, Prince Gregory came to the Tarasconian's room.

'Quick, quick, get dressed! Your Moorish lady is found. Her name is Baia. She's just twenty, and as pretty as a picture, and she's already a widow.'

'A widow! What a stroke of luck!' said the brave Tarasconian joyfully. For he was afraid of Oriental husbands.

'Yes, but she's very closely guarded by her brother.'

'Oh, hell and damnation.'

'Yes, he's a fierce fellow, this Moor. He sells pipes in the Bazaar.'

There was silence.

'Well now,' said the Prince, 'you're not the man to be frightened by a little thing like that. I dare say we can get round the ruffian by buying a few of his pipes. Come on, get dressed quickly, you old scoundrel!'

Pale and agitated, his heart bursting with love, the Tarasconian jumped out of bed, and as he hastily buttoned on his flannel breeches, he enquired: 'What ought I to do?'

'Write to the lady quite simply and ask to meet her.'

'Then she understands French?' asked the naive Tartarin with a disappointed air, for he was dreaming of the Orient pure and unalloyed.

'No, not a word,' replied the Prince imperturbably. 'But you can dictate the letter to me and I'll translate it on the spot.'

'O Prince, how very kind you are!'

And the Tarasconian began striding up and down the room, silently collecting his thoughts. Of course you cannot write to a Moorish lady in Algiers as you would to a little piece in Beaucaire. Very fortunately our hero was mindful of his varied reading, and with its aid was able to compose the most Oriental letter imaginable, an amalgam of the highflown language of Gustave Aimard's Apache warriors, and Lamartine's *Travels in the East*, with some distant memories of *The Song of Songs*. It began 'Like the ostrich in the sand,' and ended with 'Tell me the name of your father and I will tell you the name of this flower.'

The romantic Tartarin would have liked to append to this missive an emblematic bouquet of flowers in the Eastern manner. But Prince Gregory thought that it would be more valuable to buy some pipes from the brother, since this would not only sweeten the savage temper of the gentleman but would assuredly give great pleasure to the lady who smoked a great deal.

'Let's go quickly and buy some pipes,' said Tartarin full of ardour.

'No, no. Let me go alone. I shall get them cheaper.'

'What! How very kind, O Prince, Prince!' And the good man in great embarrassment handed his purse to the obliging Montenegrin, urging him not to forget anything that might give pleasure to the lady.

Unfortunately, though the affair was well begun, it did not progress as swiftly as might have been hoped. Deeply touched, it appeared, by Tartarin's eloquence, and moreover three parts won in advance, the lady would have liked nothing better than to receive Tartarin, but her brother had scruples and to calm these it was necessary to buy pipes by the dozen, by the gross, by the ship-load. 'What the devil can Baia do with all those pipes,' Tartarin sometimes wondered. But he paid for them all the same, and without haggling.

Finally, when he had bought mountains of pipes and poured forth oceans of Oriental poetry, a meeting was granted.

There is no need to describe the palpitations with which the Tarasconian prepared for it, or the fervid care with which he cut, oiled and perfumed his stiff cap-shooter's beard, without forgetting—for everything must be foreseen—to slip a spiked life-preserver into his pocket and two or three revolvers. The Prince, always obliging, came to this first assignation as interpreter. The lady lived in the upper town. Before her door, a young Moor of thirteen or fourteen was smoking cigarettes. This was the famous Ali, the brother in question. On seeing the two visitors approach, he knocked twice at the postern and discreetly retired.

The door opened. A negress appeared and without a

single word to Tartarin led the gentlemen across the narrow interior courtyard into a cool room in which the lady was waiting, reclining on a low couch. At a first glance, she appeared to Tartarin smaller and stouter than the lady of the omnibus. Was she really the same girl, indeed? This suspicion flashed though Tartarin's mind and was gone.

The lady was so pretty reclining like that with bare feet and her chubby fingers loaded with rings. She was pink and appetizing, and beneath her bodice of gold cloth, beneath the folds of her flowered dress was the suggestion of a charming creature, rather well-covered, very attractive and nicely curved all over. The amber mouthpiece of a narghile was smoking at her lips and enveloped her with a halo of white smoke.

As he entered, the Tarasconian put one hand to his heart, and bowed in the most Moorish fashion possible, rolling his large, passionate eyes. Baia looked at him for a moment without a word. Then, dropping her amber pipe-stem, she fell backwards, hiding her face in her hands. All that could be seen was her white neck convulsed with wild laughter and rippling like a bag full of pearls.

Sidi Tart'ri ben Tart'ri

If you drop into the Algerian coffee-houses of the upper town, in the early evening, even today you will hear the Moors discussing among themselves with winks and guffaws a certain Sidi Tart'ri ben Tart'ri, a very charming rich European who some years ago lived in the neighbourhood with a little local lady called Baia. This Sidi Tart'ri who has left

such happy memories around the Casbah is none other, as can be supposed, than Tartarin. And why not? There are hours of blindness, of weakness and confusion in the lives of saints and heroes, and our illustrious Tarasconian was no more immune from them than any other. And so it is that for a whole two months, forgetting glory and the lions, he was intoxicated by Eastern love and slumbered, like Hannibal at Papua, in the delights of the white city of Algiers.

The good man had rented a pretty little native house in the heart of the Arab town, with an inner courtyard, banana-palms, cool galleries and fountains, and here he lived away from all noise with his Moorish beauty, Moorish himself from head to foot, sucking all day at his narghile and eating musky sweetmeats.

Stretched on a divan in front of him, Baia, guitar in hand, would drone monotonous songs or, to amuse her lord, would dance the belly-dance, holding a small mirror in one hand in which she reflected her white teeth and made grimaces.

As the lady did not know a word of French or Tartarin a word of Arabic, conversation languished at times and the talkative Tarasconian had continually to atone for the torrents of words of which he had been guilty in Bézuquet the chemist's and at Costecalde the gunsmith's.

But even this penance was not devoid of charm, and he felt a sort of sensual perversity in staying there all day long without talking, listening to the hubble-bubble of the pipe, the plucking of the guitar and the whisper of the fountain on the mosaics of the courtyard.

The pipe, baths and love-making filled his whole life. They seldom went out. Sometimes Sidi Tart'ri, with his mistress behind him on the crupper, rode out on a stout mule to eat pomegranates in a little garden he had bought on the outskirts. But never, absolutely never did he go down into the European city. That Algiers, with its boozing Zouaves, its music-halls crowded with officers, and its perpetual clank of swords trailing under the arcades was to him as unbearable and ugly as a Western garrison town.

In short, Tartarin was very happy, Tartarin-Sancho particularly, who was very fond of Turkish sweets, and declared himself utterly satisfied with his new life. As for Tartarin-Quixote, he had some twinges at times when he thought of Tarascon and the skins he had promised. But that did not last. He had only to look at Baia or take a spoonful of one of those sweet-smelling confections, as intoxicating as Circe's draught, and they were immediately dispelled.

In the evening, Prince Gregory came to talk a little about free Montenegro. Tirelessly obliging, this pleasant nobleman filled the functions of domestic interpreter, or at need, of steward, and all for nothing, for the mere joy of it. Except for him, Tartarin entertained only Turks. All those fierce bearded brigands who had once inspired him with such fear when he saw them at the back of their dark stalls, turned out on acquaintance to be good inoffensive tradesmen, embroiderers, spice-dealers, turners of pipe stems—all well-behaved, humble, shrewd, discreet and good players at a hand of cards. Four or five times a week these gentlemen came to spend the evening with Sidi Tart'ri, won his money and ate his sweetmeats and discreetly retired on the stroke of ten giving thanks to the Prophet.

When they had gone Sidi Tart'ri and his faithful spouse finished the evening on the terrace, a large white terrace which formed the roof of the house and looked down over the town. All around them a thousand other white terraces, quiet in the moonlight, dropped down step by step to the sea. Throbbings of the guitar reached them on the wind.

Suddenly like a shower of firework stars, a loud, clear refrain would fall note by note from the sky. On the minaret of the neighbouring mosque a handsome muezzin appeared, a white shadow standing out against the deep blue of the night, and he was singing the glory of Allah in a magnificent voice that spanned the horizon.

Baia immediately dropped her guitar, and turned her large eyes towards the muezzin. They seemed to drink in the prayer voluptuously. She stayed there for the whole duration of his chant, trembling and ecstatic like an Eastern Santa Teresa. Tartarin, greatly moved, watched her pray and thought to himself that it must be a fine and powerful religion that could awake such frenzies of faith. Tarascon, hide your face, Tartarin was thinking of becoming an apostate.

News arrives from Tarascon

One fine afternoon when the sky was blue and the breeze warm, Sidi Tart'ri was returning alone from his little garden. He was riding his mule, with his legs widely straddling his large esparto-grass saddle-bags which were stuffed with citrons and water-melons. Lulled by the chink of his wide stirrups, and rocking his whole body in time with the clop-clop of the mule, the good man was riding through the charming countryside with his hands folded on his belly and three parts drugged by heat and well-being.

Suddenly as he entered the town, he was awoken by a deafening shout:

'Well, wonders will never cease! Anyone would say it was Monsieur Tartarin.' At the name of Tartarin and the cheerful accent of the Midi, the Tarasconian raised his head, to see two yards away the tanned and worthy face of Captain Barbassou, master of the *Zouave*, who was drinking an absinthe and smoking his pipe in the doorway of a small café.

'Hey! Hallo, Barbassou!' said Tartarin, stopping his mule. Barbassou gazed at him for a moment, wide-eyed, instead of answering. Then he burst out laughing so uproariously that Sidi Tart'ri fell back in confusion on to his water-melons.

'That's a fine turban, my poor Monsieur Tartarin. It's true then what they say, that you've turned Turk. How is little Baia? Does she still sing *Marco la Belle*?'

'*Marco la Belle*,' exclaimed Tartarin angrily. 'Let me tell you, Captain, that the person to whom you refer is a decent Moorish girl, and doesn't know a word of French.'

'Baia doesn't know a word of French? Where have you been all your life?' And the worthy captain began to laugh louder than ever. But when he saw poor Sidi Tart'ri's face fall, he thought better of himself.

'Perhaps it isn't the same Baia, then. Let's agree that I've made a mistake. Only, look here, Monsieur Tartarin, you'd do well to mistrust Moorish beauties and Montenegrin princes.'

Tartarin stood up in his stirrups and made an ugly face.

'The Prince is my friend, Captain.'

'All right, all right, don't get cross. Will you take an absinthe? No. No message for home, either? No. Very well. Good-bye, then. By the way, friend, I've got some good French tobacco here, if you'd like to take one or two pipefuls. Take some. You're very welcome. It will do you good. It's these damned Oriental tobaccos that have muddled your ideas.'

Tartarin found no one at home. Baia had gone to the baths. The negress seemed ugly and the house depressing. Seized by an indefinable melancholy, he sat down beside the fountain and filled a pipe with Barbassou's tobacco. The tobacco was wrapped in a scrap of the *Sémaphore*. As he unfolded it, the name of his native town leapt to his eyes: Our correspondent writes from Tarascon:

'The town is deeply disturbed. Tartarin the lion-killer, who left for Africa to hunt these beasts of Atlas, has sent no news for many months. What has become of our heroic compatriot? Knowing as we do his foolhardy enthusiasm and his thirst for adventure, we hardly dare to ask. Has he like many another been swallowed by the sands? Or has he fallen into the murderous claws of one of these monstrous felines whose skins he has promised to the municipality? There is hideous uncertainty. Some negro traders however who visited the fair at Beaucaire claim to have met deep in the desert a European whose description answers to his, and who was making for Timbuctoo. May heaven preserve our Tartarin!'

On reading this, Tartarin blushed, blanched and shivered.

All Tarascon rose before his eyes: the club, the cap-shooters, the green armchair at Costecalde's, and soaring over it all like an eagle with outspread wings, the huge moustache of the worthy Major Bravida.

Then seeing himself as he was, squatting like a coward on his mat while he was believed to be slaying wild beasts, Tartarin of Tarascon was ashamed of himself and wept.

Suddenly our hero started up: 'To the lions! To the lions!' And rushing to the dusty lumber-room in which his tent-shelter, his medicine chest, his tinned foods and his gun-case lay forgotten, he dragged them into the centre of the court. Tartarin-Sancho had just breathed his last; only Tartarin-Quixote remained.

Just a moment to inspect his stores, to arm himself, and put on his harness and his large boots, to write a few lines to the Prince, entrusting Baia to his care, and slip into the envelope some blue banknotes damp with tears, and the bold Tarasconian was travelling in a stage-coach along the Blidah highway, leaving the negress behind amazedly contemplating the narghile, turban and baggy trousers—all the Musulman accoutrements of the defrocked Sidi Tart'ri—which sprawled piteously beneath the little white trefoils of the gallery.

Third Episode

Among the Lions

Stage-coaches in Exile

It was an old stage-coach of a bygone day, upholstered in faded blue cloth with enormous coarse wool buttons which after some hours on the road ended by raising lumps on your back. Tartarin of Tarascon had an inside corner. Our hero made himself as comfortable as possible and preliminary to sniffing the rank scent of great African felines, had to content himself with the good old odour of the stage-coach, compounded of a thousand smells of men and women, horses and leather, fodder and mildewed straw.

There was a little of all sorts inside. A Trappist, some Jewish merchants, two whores returning to their regiment—the 3rd Hussars—and a photographer from Orléansville. But charming and various though the company, he was in no mood for chat and sat there brooding with his arm through the strap and his rifles between his knees. His hasty departure, Baia's dark eyes, the fearsome hunt that he was about to undertake, all these together confused his brain. And in addition this European stage-coach with its pleasantly patriarchal air, found here in the middle of Africa, vividly reminded him of the Tarascon of his youth with its horse races in the suburbs, its little dinners on the banks of the Rhône—a whole crowd of memories. Gradually night fell. The guard lit the lamps. The rusty stage-coach jolted and creaked on its old springs; the horses trotted, the bells jingled. From time to time from beneath the cover of the luggage rack there came a fearsome clanking of iron. This was the coach's armament.

Three-quarters asleep, Tartarin of Tarascon paused for a moment to view the travellers comically shaken by the jolting and dancing like grotesque shadows in front of him. Then his eyes grew dark and his thoughts hazy, and he only heard very vaguely the grinding of the wheel-hubs and the coach-panels groaning.

Suddenly a voice as of an old wicked fairy, hoarse, broken and cracked, called Tartarin by name: 'Monsieur Tartarin! Monsieur Tartarin!'

'Who's calling me?'

'It's I, Monsieur Tartarin. Don't you recognize me? I am the old coach that ran on the Nîmes–Tarascon route twenty years ago. How many times I've carried you, you and your friends when you went cap-shooting up Jonquières or Bellegarde way! I couldn't place you at first because of your Turkish fez and because you've put on a bit of weight, too. But as soon as you began snoring, God bless my soul, I recognized you in a flash.'

'That's all right. Quite all right,' said the Tarasconian, a little vexed. Then, softening again: 'But what on earth has brought you here, old girl?'

'Oh, my dear Monsieur Tartarin, I didn't come of my own free will, I assure you. Once the Beaucaire railway was finished, they could find no more use for me and so they sent me off to Africa . . . I'm not the only one. All the stage-coaches in France were deported like me. They found us too reactionary, and now we're all out here, and treated like galley-slaves. We are, what you call in France, the Algerian railways.' The old coach here heaved a long sigh before going on. 'O Monsieur Tartarin, how I miss my lovely Tarascon! That was a good time for me, when I was young. You should have seen me set out in the morning, washed with plenty of water, and all shining, with my wheels freshly varnished and my lamps like a pair of suns and my hood always freshly oiled. How lovely it was when the postillion made his whip crack to the tune of *Lagadigadaou! La Tarasque! La Tarasque!* Then the guard, with his horn slung and his embroidered cap over one ear, chucked his little dog on to the cover of the luggage rack. The dog would bark, and he would jump up after him, shouting: "Away we go! Away we go!" Then my four horses dashed off with a jingling of bells, a barking of dogs and a tune on the horn. The windows would fly open and all Tarascon would gaze with pride at the stage-coach racing out on to the great high road.

'What a lovely road it was, Monsieur Tartarin! Broad and well kept, with its mileposts and piles of stone at regular intervals, and the pretty flat fields to left and right, planted with olives and vines. Then there were inns hardly ten yards apart and relays of horses every five minutes. And what grand people my passengers were. Mayors and priests going to Nîmes to see the prefect or the bishop, taffeta-weavers returning in style from the fair, schoolboys on holiday, peasants in their embroidered smocks, freshly shaved that morning, and up above, on the roof, all of you gentlemen, the cap-shooters. You were a cheerful lot always, and you'd come back in the evenings singing under the stars, everyone his own song.

'Now, it's another story. Lord knows the people I'm carrying now! A herd of unbelievers, coming from goodness knows where and filling my cushions with vermin, negroes and Bedouins and drunks, adventurers from every country on earth, ragged settlers who poison me with their pipes and all of them talking a gibberish of which God the Father would not understand a word. And then see how they treat me!

Never brushed, never washed. They grudge me the grease for my axles. Instead of the good big calm horses of the old days, little Arab horses that have the devil inside them. They fight and bite one another and caper like goats as they run, and they shatter my shafts with their kicking. Hey! Ouch! You see? They're beginning again. And the roads! Around here they're still passable because we're near the centre of government. But out there, up country, there's nothing, there's no road at all. One takes the best way one can, over hills and plains, through the dwarf palms and the gums. Not a single fixed posting house. You stop wherever the guard fancies, sometimes at one farm and sometimes at another. Sometimes the rogue makes me run five miles out of the way, because he wants to visit a friend and drink an absinthe or an arrack. Then it's "Crack the whip, postillion. We must catch up for lost time." The sun's scorching, the dust burns you, but he whips on. We catch on the scrub, we sway. But he whips on all the harder. We swim rivers, we catch chills, we get damp, we drown. No matter. Whip on! Whip on! Then in the evening, we're dripping wet—a fine thing at my age and with my rheumatism. I have to sleep under the sky, in the courtyard of some caravanserai exposed to all the winds. At night the jackals and hyenas come to sniff my carriage-work, and marauders who are afraid of the dew come into the passenger seats to keep warm. That's the life I lead now, my poor Monsieur Tartarin, and shall always lead now till the day when I drop. Scorched by the sun and rotted by the damp nights I shall fall at some corner on this vile road, and shan't be able to save myself. Then the Arabs will come and boil their *kouskous* over the remains of my poor carcass.'

'Blidah! Blidah!' cried the guard, as he flung the door open.

A little Gentleman drops in

Vaguely, through the mud-caked glass, Tartarin of Tarascon saw the square of a pretty little minor town, a well-proportioned square surrounded by arcades and planted with orange-trees, in the middle of which toy soldiers were drilling in the thin rosy haze of morning. The cafés were taking down their shutters. In one corner was a vegetable market. It was all charming, but there was no scent of lions yet. 'To the South! To the South!' muttered Tartarin, sinking back into his corner. At this moment the door opened, and a puff of cool air came in bringing in its train, together with the sweet smell of orange-blossom, a very small gentleman in a brown frock-coat. He was old, withered, wrinkled and extremely precise. His face was no larger than a fist: he wore a black silk cravat four inches high and carried a leather brief-case and umbrella. The perfect village notary. The little gentleman sat down opposite Tartarin and seemed extremely surprised at the sight of his armaments. He stared at the Tarasconian with a tiresome persistence . . .

The horses were taken out, new horses were put in, and the coach started off. The little gentleman continued to gaze at Tartarin. Finally the Tarasconian became ruffled.

'Do my possessions surprise you?' he enquired, staring in his turn in the little gentleman's face.

'No, they are in my way,' replied the other very calmly. And indeed with his tent-shelter, his revolver, his two rifles in their case, and his hunting-knife—not to mention his natural corpulence—Tartarin of Tarascon took up a great deal of room.

The little gentleman's answer annoyed him.

'Do you by any chance imagine that I could go lion-hunting with your umbrella?' asked the great man haughtily.

The little man looked at his umbrella, smiled blandly and still completely unruffled enquired:

'Your name is then, Monsieur?'

'Tartarin of Tarascon, lion-killer.'

In pronouncing these words, the bold Tartarin shook the tassel of his fez like a mane.

Stupefaction swept through the carriage. The Trappist crossed himself, the whores uttered little frightened squeals, and the photographer from Orléansville drew closer to the lion-killer, already coveting the rare honour of taking his likeness.

The little gentleman was not put out.

'Have you killed many lions yet, Monsieur Tartarin?' he asked very calmly.

The Tarasconian received this charge with a flourish.

'Yes, I have killed a great number, sir. I only wish you had as many hairs on your head as I have killed lions.'

The whole carriage burst into laughter, as they contemplated the three yellow bristles standing up on the little gentleman's skull.

The Orléansville photographer now joined the conversation.

'A dangerous profession yours, Monsieur Tartarin. There must sometimes be some awkward moments. Poor M. Bombonnel, for example . . .'

'Oh yes, the panther-killer,' said Tartarin with some contempt.

'Do you know him then?' asked the little gentleman.

'Well good gracious me, do I know him? We have been out on the hunt together more than twenty times.'

The little gentleman smiled. 'So you hunt panther also, Monsieur Tartarin?'

'Sometimes, for amusement,' answered the furious Tarasconian.

Then lifting his head with a heroic gesture which inflamed the hearts of the two whores: 'That's nothing like lion-hunting.'

'When all's said and done,' ventured the photographer from Orléansville, 'a panther's nothing more than a big cat.'

'How right you are,' answered Tartarin who was not averse to reducing Bombonnel's glory a little, especially before these ladies.

The coach stopped, the guard came and opened the door and, addressing the old gentleman, said in a most respectful tone: 'We have arrived at your destination, sir.'

The little man rose, and got out of the coach. Then, before shutting the door, he said:

'Will you allow me to give you some advice, Monsieur Tartarin?'

'What advice, sir?'

'Now, listen. You look a decent sort of fellow. So I'd rather give it to you than not. Go back to Tarascon, Monsieur Tartarin, as quickly as you can. You're wasting your time here. There are still a few panther left in this province, but they aren't big enough game for you. But lion-hunting's finished. There are no lions left in Algeria. My friend Chassaing has just killed the last.'

Thereupon the little gentleman bowed, closed the door, and went away laughing, carrying his brief-case and his umbrella.

'Guard,' asked Tartarin, making an ugly grimace, 'who is that silly little man?'

'What, don't you know him? That's Monsieur Bombonnel that is.'

A Convent of Lions

Tartarin of Tarascon got off at Milianah, leaving the coach to continue its journey southwards. Two days of hard jolts, two nights spent open-eyed gazing through the window in hopes of seeing the huge shadow of a lion in the fields beside the road—all this sleeplessness certainly deserved a few hours' rest. Besides, if all must be told, since his misadventure with Bombonnel, the loyal Tarasconian felt ill at ease and, despite his arms, his fierce expression and his red fez, he had difficulty in facing the photographer from Orléansville and the two young ladies of the 3rd Hussars. He walked through the broad streets of Milianah, with their fine trees and fountains. As he wandered in search of a suitable hotel the poor man could not help reflecting on Bombonnel's words. Supposing they were true? What if there were no more lions in Algeria? What good would all this running about, all this exhaustion be?

Suddenly, at the turn of a street, our hero found himself face to face with—What? Guess. With a superb lion waiting before a café door, sitting there royally on its hind-quarters with its tawny mane gleaming in the sun.

'How did they dare to tell me that there weren't any more?' exclaimed Tartarin, leaping backwards. On hearing this exclamation, the lion lowered his head and, picking up in his teeth a wooden bowl which was lying on the pavement before him, humbly held it out towards Tartarin who was motionless with amazement. A passing Arab threw a copper coin into the bowl, and the lion wagged his tail. Then Tartarin understood everything. He saw what emotion had prevented him from seeing at first; the crowd, gathered around the poor tame lion, which was blind, and the two negroes armed with truncheons who were leading him through the town as an organ-grinder leads his monkey.

The Tarasconian's blood boiled in his veins. 'Wretches,' he cried in a voice of thunder, 'so to debase this noble beast.' And rushing on the lion, he snatched the ignoble bowl from between his royal jaws. Thinking that they had a thief to deal with, the two negroes fell upon Tartarin with their truncheons raised. There was a fearful shindy, the negroes smiting, some women yelping and all the children laughing. An old Jewish cobbler called from the back of his shop: 'Take him to the shushtish, take him to the shushtish.' The lion himself, in his blindness, attempted a roar, and poor Tartarin, after a desperate struggle, fell to the ground among the coppers and sweepings.

At this moment, a man forced his way through the crowd, called off the negroes with a word and the women and children with a wave of the hand. Then he picked Tartarin up, brushed him, shook him and sat him down breathless on a corner post.

'What, *Pri-ince*, is it you?' exclaimed the good Tartarin, rubbing his sides.

'Yes, my brave friend, it's I. As soon as I received your letter, I put Baia in her brother's charge, hired a post-chaise, travelled a hundred and fifty miles at top speed and here I am just in time to save you from the brutalities of these peasants. What have you been doing, in God's name, to get yourself into this trouble?'

'What do you expect, Prince? Should I look on and see this poor lion with his begging-bowl in his jaws, humiliated, conquered, mocked, and made a laughing stock by that mob of Moslems?'

'But you have made a mistake, my noble friend. The lion is on the contrary an object of respect and adoration. He is a sacred animal and a member of a great convent of lions founded three centuries ago by Mohammad-ben-Aoudah. It is like La Trappe, but wild and savage. There is no silence, only the roaring and smell of beasts. The monks are strange men. They rear and tame hundreds of lions, and send them away all over Northern Africa accompanied by begging brothers. The gifts these brothers receive go to the upkeep of this convent and its mosque. And I will tell you why the two negroes were so ill-tempered just now. They are convinced that if a copper, a single copper of the money they collect is lost through their fault, the lion they are leading will devour them on the spot.'

On hearing this improbable but truthful tale, Tartarin of Tarascon rejoiced and noisily sniffed the air.

'What pleases me most in all this,' he said by way of verdict, 'is that, whatever this fellow Bombonnel may say, there are still lions in Algeria.'

'Of course there are,' said the Prince enthusiastically. 'To-morrow we will go and beat the Shelif plain, and you'll see.'

'What's this, Prince? Is it possible that you intend to come hunting too?'

'Gracious me! Can you imagine that I mean to let you go off alone into the heart of Africa among all those savage tribes? Why, you don't know their language and you don't know their customs. No, no, my illustrious Tartarin, I shan't leave you again. Wherever you may be, I will be too.'

'Oh *Pri-ince, Pri-ince!*'

And Tartarin, beaming, pressed the valiant Gregory to his heart. He reflected with pride that like Jules Gerard, Bombonnel and all the other famous lion-hunters, he would have a foreign prince to accompany him on the chase.

The Caravan on the March

Next day, at crack of dawn, the intrepid Tartarin and the no less intrepid Prince Gregory, followed by half a dozen negro porters, left Milianah and dropped down to the plain of the Shelif along a delightful path, shaded with jasmine, eucalyptus, carobs and wild olives. On either side, behind hedges, lay little native gardens, and thousands of lively springs fell gaily from rock to rock, singing as they went. It was the sort of landscape you find in the Lebanon.

Carrying as great a weight of arms as the great Tartarin, Prince Gregory had attired himself in addition in a strange and magnificent military cap covered with gold lace, and embroidered with a wreath of oak-leaves in silver thread, which made His Highness look like a Mexican general, or the station master of some Danubian country.

This monstrous cap greatly intrigued the Tarasconian, who timidly requested some explanation.

'Indispensable headwear for travelling in Africa,' replied the Prince gravely, and shining up its peak with the back of his sleeve, he informed his credulous companion of the important part played by a military cap in relations with the Arabs. Military insignia had the sole distinction of inspiring terror in the tribesmen, and therefore the civil administration has been obliged to equip all their staff from the road inspector to the district officer in military headdress. In fact, in order to govern Algeria—the Prince is still speaking—one has no need of a good head, or even of a head at all. A military cap is enough, a grand cap gleaming with gold lace on top of a pole, like Gessler's in the story of William Tell.

Thus chatting and philosophizing, the caravan went forward. The barefooted porters leapt from rock to rock, chattering like monkeys. The gun-cases rattled, and the guns themselves glinted. The natives who passed them bowed to the earth before the magic cap. Up on the ramparts of Milianah the chief of the Arab Department was enjoying a stroll with his wife. Hearing all this unaccustomed clatter and seeing the glint of arms among the branches he thought that a revolt had broken out and raised the drawbridge. He then sounded a general alarm and put the town in a state of siege.

A fine start for the caravan!

Unfortunately before the day ended things went wrong. One of the negro porters was seized with the most frightful colic from eating the adhesive plaster in the medicine chest. Another fell dead drunk by the roadside from drinking camphorated spirits; the third, who was carrying the traveller's diary, deceived by the gilt clasps into believing that he was carrying treasure stolen from Mecca, ran off at full speed into the Zaccar.

A consultation was necessary. The caravan halted, and a council was held in the broken shade of an old fig-tree.

'My advice would be,' said the Prince, unsuccessfully trying to dissolve a pemmican tablet in an improved triple-bottomed cooking-pot, 'my advice would be that from this evening we dispense with the negro porters. There happens to be an Arab market quite close to here. The best thing will be for us to stop there and make a purchase of some donkeys.'

'No, no, not donkeys,' interrupted the great Tartarin vehemently. The memory of poor Blacky made him blush.

He added hypocritically however: 'How can you expect such small beasts to carry all our equipment?'

The Prince smiled.

'You are making a great mistake, my illustrious friend. The Algerian donkey may seem to you weak and thin, but he has a strong back. He needs it to stand the treatment he gets. Just ask the Arabs. This is how they explain our colonial organization. At the top, they say, is *Mouci* the Governor with a great stick. He beats his staff. The staff take vengeance by beating the soldiers and the soldiers beat the settlers, the settlers beat the Arabs, the Arabs beat the negroes, the negroes beat the Jews, and the Jews in their turn beat the donkeys. The poor little donkey, having no one to beat, lends his back and bears it all. So you see he can easily carry your boxes.'

'All the same,' replied Tartarin of Tarascon, 'I don't think donkeys would do. They would spoil the appearance of our caravan. I should like something more Eastern. Now if we could get a camel for instance . . .'

'As many as you like,' said His Highness. And they set out for the Arab market.

The market was held some miles away on the banks of the Shelif. There were five or six thousand tattered Arabs swarming in the sun and bargaining noisily amidst jars of black olives, pots of honey, bags of spices and large bundles of cigars. There were big fires over which they were roasting whole sheep dripping with butter. There were also open-air slaughter-houses, where naked negroes, their feet and arms red with blood, were cutting up the hanging carcasses of young goats with little knives.

In one corner, beneath a patchwork tent of a thousand colours, sat a Moorish market clerk with spectacles and a big book. Here was a group of men shouting angrily; a roulette game had been set up on a bale of wheat, and the Kabyles were at each others' throats over it. In another place there was a joyful stamping and loud laughter; they were watching a Jewish merchant and his mule drowning in the Shelif. There were scorpions, there were dogs, there were crows and flies . . . what flies!

But there were no camels. Finally they discovered one which some M'zabites were anxious to get rid of. It was a true desert camel, the classical camel, bald and sad-looking with a long Bedouin head. His hump had grown limp with long fasting, and hung dejectedly to one side.

Tartarin found him so beautiful that he desired the whole caravan to pile on his back. His Oriental fantasy was still strong.

The beast knelt and they strapped on the baggage. The Prince installed himself on the animal's neck. Tartarin for greater majesty had himself hoisted on the hump, between two boxes. Proud and well wedged in, he saluted the whole market which had gathered round, with a lofty wave of his hand. He then gave the signal to start. A devilish fine sight! If only the people of Tarascon could have seen it!

The camel got up, stretched his long knotty legs and started away.

An astounding experience. But after a few strides Tartarin felt himself turn pale, and one by one, the heroic fez resumed its positions of the time aboard the *Zouave*. This devil of a camel rolled like a man-of-war. 'Pri-ince, Pri-ince,' moaned Tartarin, deathly pale and clutching the dry tuft of the hump. 'Prince, let's get down . . . I feel . . . I feel . . . that I'm going to disgrace France.'

It was useless. The camel was well launched and nothing would stop him. Four thousand barefoot Arabs were running behind, gesticulating and laughing like mad so that their six hundred thousand white teeth glistened in the sun.

Tarascon's great man had to resign himself. He collapsed sadly on the hump. His fez took up whatever positions it fancied and France was disgraced.

The Night Ambush in a Rose-laurel Grove

Picturesque though their new mount was, the lion-slayers had to abandon it out of respect for the fez. They continued their journey therefore on foot, and the caravan went slowly south in short stages, the Tarasconian leading, the Montenegrin in the rear, and the camel in the ranks with the gun-cases. The expedition took more than a month.

Tartarin the terrible wandered for a whole month from

Arab encampment to Arab encampment across the vast plain of the Shelif searching for lions which could not be found. He crossed the huge, absurd expanse of French Algeria, where the odours of the ancient East are blended with the rank smell of absinthe and barracks. A mixture of Abraham and Zouave, part fairy-tale and part sheer burlesque, like a page of the Old Testament recited by the company sergeant or a ranker in the cavalry. A curious spectacle for eyes that could see. A wild and decayed people whom we are civilizing by teaching them our vices. The ferocious and uncontrolled rule of fantastic pashas who gravely wipe their noses on the broad ribbons of their Legion of Honour, and on the slightest excuse have their subjects beaten on the soles of their feet. The conscienceless justice of cadis in large spectacles, hypocrites who invoke the Koran and the law, who dream of the 15th of August and promotion beneath the palms, and sell their verdicts as Esau sold his birthright for a dish of lentils or sweetened *kouskous*. Debauched and sodden caids, once the batmen of some General Yussuf, who get drunk on champagne with the laundresses of Port Mahon and stuff themselves with roast mutton while, in front of their tents, the whole tribe is dying of hunger and fighting with the dogs for the scraps from their master's banquet.

All around were uncultivated plains, burnt grass, bare bushes, a scrub of cactus and gum-trees—the granary of France! A granary without grain, alas—and rich only in jackals and fleas! Abandoned encampments, frightened tribes travelling they knew not where and flying from hunger, and leaving corpses along their road. Here and there a French village with its houses in ruins, its fields unsown. The ravenous locusts had consumed everything down to the window-curtains and all the settlers were in the cafés, drinking absinthe and discussing plans for reform and a new constitution. This is what Tartarin might have seen if he had taken the trouble to look. But, entirely given up to his passion for lions, Tarascon's great son marched straight ahead, looking neither to right nor left but keeping his eyes fixed constantly on those imaginary monsters who never appeared.

As the tent-shelter steadfastly refused to open and the pemmican tablets to melt, the caravan was forced to halt at morning and evening, at tribal encampments. Thanks to Prince Gregory's cap, our travellers were welcomed everywhere with open arms. They lodged with the chieftains in their fantastic palaces, large white windowless farmhouses, in which they found, pell-mell, narghiles and mahogany sideboards, Smyrna carpets and the latest patent lamps, cedar boxes full of Turkish sequins, and statuette clocks in the style of Louis Philippe. Everywhere Tartarin was given magnificent feasts—banquets and entertainments. In his honour whole clans blazed away their powder and flashed their burnouses in the sun. Then when the powder had gone off, the worthy chieftain came and presented his bill . . . This is what is called Arab hospitality.

But still no lions. No more lions than on the Pont-Neuf in Paris. But Tartarin did not lose heart. Plunging boldly south, he spent his days trampling the scrub, poking the dwarf palms with the end of his rifle, and crying 'Frrt, frrt,' at every bush. Then every evening, before going to bed they watched in ambush for two or three hours. It was all in vain. Not a lion showed itself.

One evening however, at about six o'clock, as they were passing through a violet-coloured gum thicket, in which large quail, heavy with the heat, were tumbling about in the grass, Tartarin thought he heard—very far away, very indistinctly and much interrupted by the breeze—that marvellous roaring that he had heard so often at far-away Tarascon, from inside Mitaine's tent.

At first our hero thought that he was imagining it but the roaring began again, still distant though quite distinct. And this time it was accompanied by the howling of all the village dogs from every corner of the horizon and the rattling of the food-tins and the gun-cases against the camel's hump as the beast shivered with alarm. There was no doubt now. It was a lion. There was not a moment to lose.

Not far away was an old marabout (saint's tomb), with a white cupola and the deceased's yellow slippers placed in a niche above the door. Hanging on the walls was a mass of strange and miscellaneous offerings, scraps of cloaks, gold thread and red hair. Tartarin of Tarascon posted his prince and his camel here, and himself went off in search of a good ambush. Prince Gregory wanted to follow him, but the Tarasconian refused to allow him. He was bent on confronting the lion in single combat. Nevertheless he besought His Highness not to go far away, and as a precautionary measure entrusted him with his wallet. It was a fat one and full of valuable papers and banknotes, and he was afraid that these might be scattered by the lion's claw. Having done this, the hero sought his post. A hundred yards in front of the marabout, on the edge of an almost dry stream, a little grove of rose-laurels trembled in the twilight breeze. Here Tartarin took up his post, one knee on the ground, according to the rule, and clutching his carbine. His huge hunting-knife was planted boldly in front of him, in the sand of the river-bank.

Night fell. The rosy hue of nature turned to violet, then to dark blue. Down among the pebbles of the stream-bed a little pool of clear water shone like a mirror. This was the animals' drinking-place. On the slope of the further bank the white path that their great paws had traced through the scrub could vaguely be seen. This mysterious slope made him shiver. Add to this the ill-defined pullulation of African nights, the swishing of branches, the velvet tread of marauding animals, the shrill howl of the jackal, and up in the sky, three or four hundred feet aloft, vast flocks of cranes passing and crying like children having their throats cut, there was every reason why a man should feel disturbed.

Tartarin was disturbed. Indeed he was most disturbed. The poor man's teeth were chattering and the muzzle of his small-bore rifle rattled like a pair of castanets on the guard of his hunting-knife. What would you expect? There are evenings when one is not in the mood; and moreover where would the merit be if heroes were never afraid?

Well, Tartarin was certainly afraid, and all the time too. Nevertheless he stuck to his post for an hour, even for two. But heroism has its limits. Near him, in the dry bed of the stream, Tartarin suddenly heard the noise of steps and rolling pebbles. Now terror raised him from the ground; he fired two shots at random into the night and retired at full speed to the marabout, leaving his knife upright in the sand as a cross commemorating the most awful panic that ever assailed the soul of a conqueror of dragons.

'Help, help, Prince, the lion!' Silence. 'Prince, Prince, are you there?'

The Prince was not there. Alone in the moonlight the good camel threw the strange shadow of his hump on the white wall of the marabout. Prince Gregory had slipped off taking the wallet full of banknotes. His Highness had been waiting a whole month for this opportunity.

At last

It was not until early on the day that followed this adventurous and tragic evening that our hero awoke and made certain that the Prince and the cash had indeed irremediably disappeared. Seeing himself alone on this little white tomb, betrayed, robbed, deserted in the middle of savage Africa, with a one-humped camel and a handful of small change as his only resources, then for the first time the Tarasconian doubted. He had doubts of Montenegro, he had doubts of friendship, he doubted glory, he even doubted lions; and like Christ on Gethsemane this great man began to weep bitterly.

Now whilst he was sitting thoughtfully, with his head in his hands, before the door of the marabout, his rifle between his knees, and beneath the gaze of the camel, suddenly the shrubs parted before him, and Tartarin saw to his amazement a gigantic lion looming ten yards in front of him. The beast advanced with head high and emitting mighty roars which made the walls of the marabout shake beneath their votive knick-knacks, and even the saint's slippers tremble in their niche.

The Tarasconian alone did not tremble. 'At last,' he cried, jumping up and pressing the rifle butt to his shoulder. 'Bang, bang! Pfft, pfft!' It was all over, the lion had two explosive bullets in his head. For a moment there was a fearful firework display of brains and splashes of streaming blood, and scattered tawny mane against the molten background of the African sky. Then all fell quiet again and Tartarin saw . . . Two huge angry negroes rushing at him brandishing their cudgels. The two negroes of Milianah! Alas, it was the tame lion, the poor blind lion of Mohammad's convent. It was this lion that the Tarasconian bullets had just slain. This time, by the beard of the Prophet, Tartarin had a lucky escape. Beside themselves with fanatical fury the two negro alms collectors would assuredly have beaten him to pulp, if the God of the Christians had not sent a delivering angel to his aid. The rural guard of the commune of Orléansville came down the little path with his sword under his arm.

The sight of the municipal cap promptly calmed the negroes' fury. Peaceably and majestically, the man with the badge composed an interlocutory account of the affair, had the lion's remains loaded on the camel, ordered the plaintiffs and the delinquent to follow him and set off for Orléansville, where the information was lodged with the clerk of the court.

It was a long and fearful case. Having wandered through tribal Algeria, Tartarin now made the acquaintance of another Algeria no less terrifying and absurd, urban Algeria, litigious and pettifogging. He came to know the crooked judge who does his business at the back of the café, the Bohemia of the legal gentry, he became familiar with papers stinking of absinthe, and white cravats spotted with arrack. He met ushers, attorneys, all those lean and hungry stamped-paper locusts who consume the settler to the uppers of his boots and leave him plucked like a maize-plant, leaf by leaf. The first thing to be ascertained was whether the lion had been killed on civil or military territory. In the former case the matter rested with the commercial court: in the latter Tartarin would face a court martial, and at the mere name the impressionable Tarasconian already saw himself shot at the foot of the ramparts, or huddled in the depths of a fortress cell.

The awful thing is, that the delimitation of these two territories is very vague in Algeria. In fact after a month of running about, intriguing and sitting in the sun in the courtyards of the Arab Department, it was established that though on the one hand the lion had been killed on military territory, Tartarin on the other hand had been on civil territory when he fired. The case therefore rested with the civil court, and our hero got off for a *fine of two thousand five hundred francs*, exclusive of costs.

How was he to pay all that? The few piastres that had escaped the Prince's sweep had gone long ago on legal papers and judicial absinthe. The unfortunate lion-slayer was therefore reduced to selling his case of guns singly, carbine by carbine. He sold his knives, his Malayan kris, his life-preservers. A grocer bought his tinned foods, a chemist what remained of his adhesive plasters. His great hunting-boots also departed as did his patent tent-shelter to a dealer in bric-à-brac who promoted them to the rank of curiosities from Cochin China. When his debts were paid, Tartarin had nothing left but the lion's skin and the camel. He packed the skin carefully and addressed it to Tarascon, to the house of the worthy Major Bravida. (We shall see in a moment what became of this fabulous trophy.) As for the camel, he proposed to use it as a means of getting back to Algiers, not on its back but by selling it to pay his coach-fare: which is the best way of making a camel carry you. Unfortunately the beast was hard to dispose of, and no one offered a penny for it.

Tartarin wanted to get back to Algiers at all costs. He was eager to see Baia's blue jacket again, and his little house and its fountains, and to rest on the white trefoils of his little cloister while he waited for money to come from France. So our friend did not hesitate; distressed but not downcast, he planned to make the journey on foot, without money and in short stages.

In this undertaking the camel did not abandon him. This strange animal had taken an inexplicable liking to his master, and on seeing him leave Orléansville marched dutifully behind him, suiting his pace to Tartarin's and never straying a yard from him. At the beginning, Tartarin found this devotion touching. The beast's fidelity against all odds stirred his heart, especially as he was accommodating and lived on nothing. After several days however the Tarasconian became bored at having this melancholy companion perpetually on his heels. He reminded him of all his disasters. Then bitterness intervening, he hated the creature for his sad look, his hump and his bridled goose's gait. In the end he came to loathe the faithful beast, and only wished to be rid of him, but the camel stuck to him. Tartarin tried to lose him, but the camel found him again; he tried running, but the camel ran faster. He shouted 'Get out' and flung stones at him. The camel stopped and looked at him sadly, then after a moment continued on his way and always finished by catching him up. Tartarin had to resign himself.

However when after eight long days on the road the weary and dusty Tarasconian saw the first flat roofs of

Algiers gleaming far off in the greenery, when he found himself on the edge of the city among the Zouaves, the drinking-shops and the laundresses on the noisy Avenue Mustapha and they all swarmed around him watching him and his camel march past, Tartarin's patience once and for all deserted him: 'No, no,' he said to himself, 'this is impossible. I can't enter Algiers with an animal like this.' Taking advantage of a congestion of traffic he turned off into the fields and leapt into a ditch. After a moment he looked up and saw the camel striding rapidly down the highway, his neck extended in anxious concern.

Then relieved of a great weight, our hero came out of his hiding-place and re-entered the city by a roundabout path which ran under the wall of his own little garden.

Disaster upon Disaster

On reaching his Moorish villa Tartarin stopped in great astonishment. Day was dying and the street was deserted. Through the low arched doorway, which the negress had forgotten to close, he heard laughter, the chink of glasses and the popping of champagne corks. And above all this din, he heard a woman's voice singing gaily and clearly:

> Marco la belle, Marco la belle,
> You're the belle of the flowery ball,
> Don't you love it, Marco la Belle,
> Swinging the length of the flowery hall?

'Good God Almighty,' exclaimed Tartarin, turning pale. And he dashed into the courtyard. Unlucky Tartarin! What a spectacle awaited him. Under the arcade of the little cloister, amidst bottles, cakes, scattered cushions, pipes, tambourines and guitars, stood Baia, without her blue jacket or her bodice. Clad only in a silver gauze shift, and wide pale pink trousers, she was singing *Marco la Belle* with a ship's officer's cap tilted over one ear. On a rug at her feet, gorged with love and sweetmeats, Barbassou, the infamous Captain Barbassou was bursting with laughter as he listened.

The appearance of Tartarin, lean, haggard, dusty, his eyes aflame and his fez bristling, cut this pleasing Turco-Marseillais orgy short. Baia gave the shrill shriek of a frightened rabbit and vanished into the house. But Barbassou was not upset; he laughed even louder:

'Hey, hey, Monsieur Tartarin, what do you say to this? You see, she can speak French.'

Tartarin of Tarascon advanced in a fury: 'Captain!'

'Tell 'em what 'appened, pal,' cried the Moorish girl, leaning over the first-floor gallery in a pretty roguish attitude. The poor man collapsed, overwhelmed, on a drum. His Moorish girl even spoke with a Marseilles accent.

'Didn't I tell you not to trust an Algerian girl?' observed Captain Barbassou sententiously. 'Same thing as your Montenegrin prince.'

Tartarin raised his head.

'Do you know where the Prince is?'

'Oh, he's not far away. For the next five years he'll be in that handsome Mustapha prison. The rogue let them catch him red-handed. But it's not the first time he has been put away. His Highness has already done three years inside somewhere or other. Just a moment though, I think it was at Tarascon.'

'At Tarascon!' cried Tartarin, suddenly enlightened. 'So that's why he only knew one side of the town.'

'No doubt. Tarascon seen from the town gaol. Oh my poor Monsieur Tartarin, you have to keep your eyes very wide open in this devilish country. Or else very unfortunate things are liable to happen to you. Your experience, for instance, with the muezzin.'

'What experience? What muezzin?'

'Eh? Goodness me! The muezzin opposite of course, who is making up to Baia. The story was in the local paper the other day, and the whole town's still laughing over it. He's a sly fellow, that muezzin! While chanting up there on his tower, he was making declarations to the girl right under your nose. He would call on the name of Allah and make an appointment with her, all at the same time!'

'Is everybody a rogue in this country?' shrieked the unhappy Tartarin.

Barbassou gave a philosophic shrug.

'These new countries, you know, my dear fellow. But never mind. If you take my advice you'll go back pretty quickly to Tarascon.'

'Go back? That's easily said. But what about the money? You don't know how they robbed me, down there in the desert.'

'Don't worry about that,' said the Captain, laughing. 'The *Zouave*'s leaving tomorrow and I'll take you if you want to come. Does it suit you, chum? Very well then. There's only one more thing for you to do. There are still a few bottles of champagne left and half a pie. Sit down there and forget all your grudges.'

After a moment's hesitation which his dignity demanded

the Tarasconian made a manful decision. He sat down and they drank a toast. Baia, who had come down when she heard their glasses, sang the last verses of *Marco la Belle* and the feast went on late into the night.

Towards three in the morning, with a light head but a heavy foot, Tartarin, returning from escorting his friend the Captain home, passed the mosque, and the memory of the muezzin and his tricks made him laugh. Immediately a fine idea for vengeance came into his head. The door was open, he went in and down long corridors hung with mats. He climbed the stairs and went on climbing till he finally found himself in a little Turkish prayer-room, in which a pierced iron lantern swung from the ceiling, patterning the white walls with strange shadows.

The muezzin was there, sitting on a divan, in his great turban and white robe. He was smoking his long pipe, and before him was a large glass of cool absinthe which he was stirring religiously while awaiting the hour for calling the faithful to prayer. At the sight of Tartarin he dropped his pipe in terror.

'Not a word, parson,' said the Tarasconian who had his plan. 'Quick, your turban, and your robe.' The Turkish priest, trembling, gave him his turban, his smock, anything he liked. Tartarin robed himself and walked gravely on to the terrace of the minaret.

The sea gleamed in the distance. The white roofs sparkled in the moonlight. A few belated guitars sounded on the sea breeze. The muezzin of Tarascon momentarily collected himself, then lifting his arms he began to intone in a very shrill voice:

'La Allah il Allah. Mahomet is an old cheat. The East, the

Koran, the pashas, lions and Moorish beauties, they aren't worth a bent halfpenny. There are no more *Turks*. There's nothing left but twisters. Long live Tarascon! Tarascon for ever!'

And whilst the illustrious Tartarin flung his cheerful curses to the four quarters—the town, the sea, the plain and the mountain—in his strange mixture of Arabic and Provençal, the other muezzins answered him in clear and solemn tones, from minaret to minaret into the far distance, and the last of the faithful in the upper town devoutly beat their breasts.

Tarascon! Tarascon!

At midday the *Zouave* was getting up steam, ready to start. Up on the balcony of the Café Valentin, the officers were levelling their telescope and from the Colonel downwards in order of rank, taking a look at the little ship setting out for France. This was the great entertainment of the garrison officers. Down below, the anchorage sparkled. The breeches of the old Turkish cannon cemented into the waterfront shone in the sun. The passengers hurried aboard. Biskris and Minorcans piled their luggage on to the lighters.

As for Tartarin of Tarascon, he had no luggage. He strolled down the Rue de la Marine, through the little market full of bananas and water-melons, accompanied by his friend Barbassou. The unfortunate Tarasconian had left his case of guns and his illusions on the Barbary shore and now he was hastening to sail for Tarascon, with his empty hands in his pockets. He had barely leapt into the Captain's cutter when a panting animal slid down from the square above and rushed towards him at a gallop. It was the camel, the faithful camel which for the past twenty-four hours had been searching Algiers for his master.

On seeing him Tartarin changed colour and pretended not to recognize him. But the camel persisted. He bounded along the quay. He called his friend, he gazed at him affectionately. 'Take me with you,' his sad eye seemed to say, 'take me in that ship far, far from this sham Arabia, this absurd Orient full of locomotives and stage-coaches. There is no place for a dromedary here. I do not know what I can turn to. You are the last Turk, I am the last camel. My dear Tartarin, let us stick together.'

'Is that camel yours?' asked the Captain.

'Certainly not,' replied Tartarin, who shuddered at the idea of entering Tarascon in such ridiculous company. Impudently denying the companion of his misfortunes, he cast the soil of Algeria from his foot, and pushed the cutter off from the landing-stage. The camel sniffed the water, stretched his neck, made his joints crack and plunged in behind the cutter. He swam for safety towards the *Zouave* with the hump on his back floating like a gourd, and his long neck stretched on the water like the beak of a galley. Cutter and camel reached the side of the steamer at the same time.

'I'm really sorry for that dromedary,' said Captain Barbassou with emotion. 'What I'd like to do is to take him aboard. When we get to Marseilles I'll make a gift of him to the Zoo.'

So with a great assemblage of blocks and tackle they hoisted the camel, now heavy with the weight of water, on to the deck, and the *Zouave* put out to sea.

Tartarin spent the two days of the crossing alone in his cabin. It was not because the seas were rough or the fez suffered too badly, but because that confounded camel paid his master the most ridiculous attentions every time he came on deck. Never did a camel make such an exhibition of a man before.

Every now and then Tartarin put his nose to the port-hole of the cabin; hourly he saw the blue of the Algerian sky fade. Then one morning to his delight, he heard all the bells of Marseilles ring out together through a silvery mist. They had arrived. The *Zouave* cast anchor.

Having no luggage, our man got off without saying a word. He walked hurriedly through Marseilles always in fear that the camel might be following him. He did not take breath till he was installed in a third-class carriage on the train to Tarascon. But he was in a fool's paradise. They were no more than five miles from Marseilles when all heads hung out of the windows. There were cries of astonishment. Tartarin looked out also . . . and what did he see? The camel, sir, the inevitable camel racing along the rails behind the train, across the desolate plain, and keeping up with it. Tartarin sank back into his corner in horror, and closed his eyes.

After his disastrous expedition, Tartarin had intended to slip home incognito. But the presence of this tiresome quadruped made this impossible. What sort of triumphal entry would this be? Lord help us! Without a halfpenny and not a lion, nothing . . . absolutely nothing except a camel! 'Tarascon! Tarascon!' He must get down.

Good gracious! No sooner did the hero's fez appear at the carriage window, than a great shout of 'Long live Tartarin' made the glass roof of the station rattle. 'Long live Tartarin

the lion-slayer!' There was a fanfare of horns and the choirs of the local musical societies burst into song. Tartarin felt like death; he believed it was a hoax. But it was not. All Tarascon was there, waving their hats in affectionate welcome. There was the good Major Bravida, Costecalde the gunsmith, the President, the chemist, and the whole noble body of cap-shooters. They crowded round their chief and carried him in triumph down the station stairs.

Strange are the effects of the mirage! The blind lion's skin which Tartarin had sent to Bravida was the cause of all this uproar. That humble pelt, exhibited to the club, had flown to the heads of all Tarascon, and their exhilaration had infected the whole South. The *Sémaphore* had discussed it. A dramatic story had been invented. Tartarin had not slain merely one lion. He was now credited with ten, twenty . . . he had made mincemeat of the lions. So when Tartarin disembarked at Marseilles, he was famous without knowing it, and an enthusiastic telegram had arrived at his native town two hours before him.

But what brought popular rejoicing to a climax was the sight of a fantastic animal, covered with dust and sweat, which appeared behind the hero and clip-clopped down the station stairs. For a moment Tarascon believed that its local dragon had come again.

But Tartarin reassured his fellow-citizens. 'That's my camel,' he observed. And already under the influence of the Tarasconian sun, that lovely sun which breeds such innocent lies, he added, patting the dromedary's hump: 'He's a noble beast. He saw me kill all my lions.'

Thereupon Tartarin seized the Major's arm in a friendly grip and Bravida blushed with pleasure. Followed by his camel, surrounded by the cap-shooters and acclaimed by the whole populace, Tartarin of Tarascon then quietly walked home to the house of the baobab, and as he walked he began the story of his great hunting expeditions:

'Imagine me now,' he began, 'on a certain evening, just as night was falling, out in the depths of the Sahara . . .'